ANOTHER SIDE OF ZOË

By Shannon Yarbrough

Another Side of Zoë

For Lois

The one I miss most from Memphis

"Don't worry about a thing,
'cause every little thing gonna be alright."

-Bob Marley

Chapter 1

It had been another slow business day at Hands Across The Board, but Zoë was exhausted. Hands Across The Board was the name of her art shop in historic Overton Square in Midtown Memphis.

The shop was a melting pot of all types of art made by local artists: pottery, jewelry, paintings, sculptures, and lots of photography. Anyone from the city could sell their art there for a commission. Artists made sixty percent, and Zoë kept forty. It was a decent arrangement when things were selling.

Over the years Zoë had taken on many roles at the shop. She was no longer just an art curator and businesswoman. She was a host every time an artist had an open house at the shop. She was a caterer because she would prep all the food and drinks for the events to save money unless the artist paid for a caterer, and they *never* paid for a caterer. Since she was the only employee at the shop, she was the manager, cashier, accountant, and janitor too.

Recently, on slow days like today, she'd taken on the role of therapist. Some of the regulars would stop by to see what pieces they'd sold. Since the shop wasn't busy, they'd stay and fill her in on all their woes, asking her for advice on anything from whether or not they should get a part-time job to if they should go on the pill. Others were depressed, dealing with drug addictions, lonely, or debating on how and when to come out to their parents.

Lately, they'd all been disappointed because nothing was selling except for some black and white photographs of town landmarks that a photographer had turned into postcards to appeal to tourists. He even bought a spinner rack for the postcards and asked Zoë if he could install it. It didn't take up much room, so she let him. He had to restock the display at least once a month.

"I bet you're glad to be selling something, right? I mean he's probably single-handily keeping the doors open for the rest of us, isn't he?" one young girl said in regards to the postcards. She sold framed sketches on post-its.

"Ha! No," Zoë said.

"But he constantly sells out."

"Sixty, Forty. Do the math," Zoë said.

The girl's mouth fell open, and she rolled her eyes up to the ceiling, apparently attempting math.

"He charges three dollars per postcard," Zoë said.

Silence.

"Forty percent is a dollar twenty."

"Oh. How much do you make from my stuff?"

"Right now, zero."

"Should I charge less?"

Zoë didn't have the heart to tell her that no one wanted a framed post-it with a water-color kitten on it. Right now, customers just wanted postcards of Graceland and Beale Street. All the artists wanted advice and wanted Zoë to tell them how they could sell more.

"Should I change my medium?"

"What should I paint?"

"Should I learn how to sew? Tons of people sew stuff on Etsy."

"What would you do?" they all asked.

Zoë didn't know the answers to their questions, so she always told each of them the same thing:

"Give it time. You'll find your way."

She didn't mind the company of artists. She thought of the

younger ones as her children, and she wanted to be there for them. They never cared if they sold a thing. They were just happy that someone was willing to show their work.

They'd even bring their parents in and show them their pieces hanging on the shop wall. Moms would take out their cell phones and make their kids stand in front of their work so they could take a pic. The shop would light up with their smiles, and moments like these reminded Zoë why she'd opened this place.

A struggling artist was like a homeless person or a stray cat to her. They spoke to her heart, and she wanted to take time to do something for them. She knew her shop was the shelter they needed to stay out of the rain, and she was the caregiver. The world needed more of that. The world needed more smiles created out of proud parents and art.

The problem was Zoë gave good advice, but she didn't follow it. She'd lost her way. She'd lost her smile. Their lengthy, daily visits sure helped pass the day, but she was growing tired of not making any money. She was growing tired of her roles as a cheerleader, advice giver, and listener.

Chapter 2

Seraphina was a professional listener. She called herself a "professional" at several things, always picking up regular odd jobs from the extremely wealthy and more affluent society about town. She did not clean houses. She did not walk dogs. She did not babysit children; she despised children. Seraphina was a regular "Girl Friday."

Mrs. Adelman needed a personal assistant to help plan and organize her son's bar mitzvah. She called Seraphina. Mrs. Adelman got her number from the Goldmans who had hired Seraphina to decorate and plan their annual Christmas gala. They'd called Seraphina after attending the Haggerty's 50th wedding anniversary at the Moose Lodge. Not only had Seraphina planned the evening, but she'd also organized the guest list, mailed the invitations, and helped Mrs. Haggerty with the seating chart after her daughter got food poisoning. When Mrs. Haggerty's manicurist had overbooked, Seraphina sat down and filed her nails and gave her a coat of Crimson.

"Red, Seraphina?" Mrs. Haggerty said, pulling back her hand.

"Let everyone know you're a fiery one," Seraphina replied with confidence.

"You're the fiery one! You're an angel. I don't know what I'd do without you."

Fiery one? Seraphina liked that. She liked it so much she put it on a business card. She had a business card for every occasion: stylist, counselor, event planner, shopper, personal assistant, professional organizer, beauty consultant, and more. *She's a fiery one!* was printed in gold foil across the bottom of her event planner and stylist cards.

Shopping was her forté. Need to pick the perfect baby shower gift? Call Seraphina. Need new furniture for the lake house? Call Seraphina. New linens and place settings for twelve for the annual Labor Day soiree? Call Seraphina. Forgot a birthday gift? You know what to do.

Seraphina once delivered a brand new silk tie to the Foresters after Mr. Forester spilled wine on his at dinner before they'd gone to the Orpheum Theatre. They'd made it in time for their front row seats for "Phantom," and Seraphina had even brought along a bottle of club soda and used it to remove a small wine stain from Mr. Forester's collar.

When she had an evening to herself, she liked to go dancing at the Time Out Club, a funky disco joint south of downtown. She could always use a cocktail, a disco ball, and some time out.

"What's your name?" a man said to her on the light-up dance floor. He was a tall drink of hot chocolate with a chiseled chest, shaved head, and arms twice as big as her thighs.

"Seraphina."

"Can I call you Sera?"

"No."

"Can I call you Phina?"

"No."

"Can I call you?" he said, holding his hand up to the side of his head and mimicking a telephone.

Seraphina rolled her eyes. She held her hands in front of her and mimicked texting on a cell phone. He laughed, took out his cell, and handed it to her. She put her number in his contacts and entered her name all in caps: SERAPHINA!

"Is this your real number?" he asked, looking at his phone.

"Find out," she said and walked off the dance floor.

She went to the ladies room and was just about to reapply her lip gloss when she heard her cell phone ding from inside her purse. She checked it, and there was one new text message:

Hi SERAPHINA! I'm Kyson. Buy you a drink?

No thanks.

Not interested?

No. Sorry.

☹

ACK! Wait…not what I meant…

LOL

Drink = No. Interested = Yes.

☺

It wasn't a habit for her to go home with men, especially ones she met at Time Out, and especially on the first night. Who was she kidding? It wasn't a habit for her to meet, much less even see men as hot as Kyson at Time Out on any night for that matter. She wanted to see his bare chest. Who was she kidding? She wanted to feel that bare chest pressed against her.

They went to her place. He was still a stranger, and at least she'd be in her comfort zone. She wasn't worried. Her neighbor was a cop; and her roommate, a loaded S&W .357 revolver, was in her nightstand.

Kyson turned out to be a true gentleman, and his rock hard

abs and massive pecs were worth leaving the light on. It was his cheetah-print bikini thong that caught her off guard. He wasn't wearing it for very long because they went straight to the bedroom, but he put it back on when they were done. He also put his tee shirt back on.

What man puts a thong back on to go to sleep?

Chapter 3

Alexandra was a walking streak of turbans and taffeta. She floated into Hands Across The Board carrying a pot of bright yellow and red zinnias from her garden. She liked to be called Zandy. Not Sandy with an S. Zandy with a Z. Just like Liza, but because Sandy with an S "sounded beachy." Zoë thought Zandy with a Z sounded bitchy. She couldn't believe this woman had given birth to her.

"These are for you," Zandy said, handing the flowers to Zoë.

"Are you going to a funeral, Mama?"

"Maybe. This place smells dead."

Zoë stuck her nose in the air and sniffed.

"New perfume?" she asked her mom.

"No. I just thought this place could use a pop of color."

"I'd like to pop you upside the head with this pot," Zoë said under her breath.

With one hand on her hip and the other clutching her chin, Zandy looked around and judged the place with her heavy eyes. Zoë put the zinnias on the counter. She turned back to the book she was reading and ignored her mother as she walked around the shop and feigned interest in the artwork. It was a routine Zoë was quite accustomed to by now.

"What is this?" Zandy said, holding up a piece of pottery.

"It's a vase," Zoë said, looking up from her book.

"It looks like a dildo."

"It's whatever you want it to be."

"I didn't say I wanted it to be a dildo. I just said it looks like one."

Zoë ignored her.

"When did you get these?"

She'd found the black and white postcards on the spinner rack.

"A year ago."

Zandy laid three of the postcards on the counter.

"You bought this one last week, Ma," Zoë said, holding up a postcard of the Hernando de Soto Bridge.

"Fine, I'll put it back. I was just trying to help," she said, putting the postcard back on the rack.

"By buying three postcards?"

"You want to go to lunch?" Zandy asked.

"No."

"You want to go to the casino with me tonight?"

"Yes."

"Pick you up at three."

She put six dollar bills on the counter and walked out, apparently immune to paying tax, but Zoë didn't mind. Despite their cattiness with each other, she knew her mom meant well so she never said anything, and the flowers were nice. Zandy knew zinnias were Zoë's favorite flower.

Chapter 4

When her mom said she'd pick Zoë up at three, she meant three in the morning. Zoë had not seen a customer or artist all day, so she closed shop an hour early. She could go home and eat dinner, take a relaxing hot bath, and then grab a few hours of sleep before waking up and getting dressed for the casino.

She put on a long silk-print skirt and a Bob Marley tee-shirt. She knew her mom would pay for everything, but she dumped some change from her piggy bank into a plastic bag and put it in her purse hoping to put some of it to good use on the penny slots.

Zandy liked to go to the casino in the early morning on a

weekday because it was not as crowded. She also claimed it paid out for her better during that time, which was true since she rarely came home empty-handed. From a couple of hundred dollars to a couple of thousand, if Zoë went with her she'd share her winnings, knowing that Zoë needed to pay her bills and buy groceries.

Zandy picked up Zoë in her boyfriend's Lincoln Town Car. It was a giant boat of a car but clean and roomy inside with its red leather interior and token fuzzy dice hanging from the mirror.

Zandy's boyfriend was named Frampton. He liked to go to the casino too, but not at three in the morning. Frampton had been Zoë's father's best friend since junior high. When her father got terminal lung cancer, he made Frampton promise he'd take care of Zandy and Zoë.

But it was Zandy who'd taken care of Frampton instead. He'd lost his job and become homeless, so she'd taken him in. Over time, they'd become more than friends. Zoë didn't care about that as long as Frampton was good to her. They both deserved happiness.

"Where's Frampton?" Zoë said, getting in the car.

"You know damn well where he is. Home in bed passed out."

"Hennessy?"

"Is it Tuesday already?"

"Technically, it's Wednesday," Zoë said.

"It was Monday when he started."

"He's going to ruin his liver."

"I don't think he has one."

"Aren't you worried about him drinking so much?"

"Nope. If his hands are groping the bottle, they aren't groping me."

"You guys aren't having sex?"

"Not with him, I'm not."

"With who then?"

"Not who. What!"

"Now I know why you asked if that vase was a dildo."

"Zoë! Don't you worry. Me and Frampton are good. I do like his car."

"I like his car too," Zoë said, reclining the seat and lying back to relax. She'd catch a nap or two while they sailed down the highway to the casinos in Tunica, Mississippi.

Chapter 5

Zandy left Zoë to go to the roulette tables. Zoë went straight for the slots. She quickly discovered the machines no longer took coins, only bills. The cashier wouldn't take her zip lock bag of pennies unless they were rolled.

"What casino turns down money?" Zoë asked in disbelief.

The cashier ignored her. With no money, she walked through the casino to find her mom.

"Done already?" Zandy said when Zoë appeared next to her.

"Haven't started."

Zandy held up two twenties. Zoë took them and walked away.

Zoë cashed a twenty for all ones so she could tip the cocktail waitresses. Drinks were free as long as you were playing. She put the other twenty in a penny slot and sat down. It didn't take long for her to get a Rum and Coke. An hour and four cocktails later, she'd tripled her money, but had played off a third of her winnings when Zandy showed up.

"Want to get something to eat?"

"Sure, let me cash out."

"Win anything?"

"Nope, but I didn't lose anything either."

"Broke even?"

"It's your money so I'm definitely broke."

She handed the forty dollar note to Zandy, but she waved it off.

"Keep it. I didn't say we were done."

The casino had a twenty-four hour diner. They sat down and ordered their usual casino breakfast. Zandy got shrimp and grits with coffee. Zoë ordered a loaded omelet and a Bloody Mary.

"Drink much?"

"Yep," Zoë said, chewing on the dill pickle that had come in her drink.

"Guess I'll be driving us home?"

"You'd let me drive Frampton's car?"

"Nope."

"I can't believe the machines don't take coins. My purse is so heavy," Zoë said.

"What do you have in there?"

Zoë took out the bag of coins and plopped it on the table. Zandy rolled her eyes.

"I'm not taking this home," Zoë said.

"What are you going to do with it?"

"I got the tip!"

She opened the bag and dumped the coins on the table.

After breakfast, they went back to their posts. Zoë decided to switch from Rum and Coke to black coffee to sober up a bit. She knew she could sleep it off during the ride home. She took a chance on the quarter slots and was up two hundred dollars when Zandy appeared again with a smile on her face.

"Time to go?" Zoë asked.

"Mama needs her beauty sleep."

"How much is Mama sleeping on tonight?"

"Four thousand."

"You won four thousand dollars?!"

"Shhh. Not so loud. How did you do?"

"Two hundred."

They cashed out and counted their money before leaving the cashier's stand. Zandy handed half to Zoë.

"Ma? You're giving this to me?" Zoë tried to act surprised, but they'd gone through this charade many times. Zandy always gave her half.

"You don't want it?"

"I didn't say that."

Zoë took the stack of bills, folded it in half, and tucked it under her bra strap.

"You want half of my winnings?" Zoë asked, teasing.

Zandy ignored her.

Chapter 6

"Girl! He gay!" Zoë screeched.

"Believe me! He ain't gay." Seraphina said.

Seraphina was Zoë's best friend. They'd met twenty years ago when Zoë first opened Hands Across The Board. Seraphina had come in looking for some interesting art pieces to decorate a client's downtown condo. They immediately clicked and had been inseparable ever since.

Anytime Seraphina needed art, she called Zoë. Today, Seraphina was treating Zoë to lunch at the Rum Boogie Café on Beale so she could tell her all about her night with Kyson.

"What straight man wears a bikini thong?" Zoë asked.

"Girl, I don't know. A stripper maybe?"

"A gay stripper! What straight man wears a cheetah print bikini thong?"

"He ain't gay!"

"He put the thong back on and went to sleep!"

"That is weird, isn't it?"

"Was it small?"

"What? The thong?"

"Yeah."

"I've blown my nose on tissues that were bigger."

"What a waste of fabric."

"It definitely left little to the imagination. Well, not little."

They both cackled.

"Are you going to see him again?" Zoë asked.

"His abs alone would be worth another look. And that butt! Damn! Boy got a booty!"

"If you change your mind, give him my number."

"How was the casino with Zandy? Win big?" Seraphina asked.

"Mom did."

"Did she share?"

"I wouldn't go if she didn't."

Because of Zandy and Seraphina, Zoë had managed to keep Hands Across The Board afloat the last few years, but things weren't improving. Zandy was getting older, and Zoë had noticed her trips to the casino were becoming fewer. And Seraphina's need for artwork was even more intermittent.

"How's things at the shop?" Seraphina asked, which was her polite way of asking if the recent trip to the casino had helped.

"You know I love having my own small business, but that's the problem. It's too small. I've always had rough patches, but now I go entire weeks without a sale. Ma's money is nice, but it's not always going to be there."

"Let me call some clients, see what I can do."

"Girl, I appreciate it. I really do, but it's not going to be enough. Some of the problem is me. I used to love to go into work every day. Now some days feel like a chore and I don't want to be there."

"Take a vacation."

"I can't afford to!"

"I'll pay. You can go with me We'll go to the beach. Or New York. How about New Orleans?"

"Girl! Stop! It's not just me. Some of it is the artists too. They drag me down. They get mad because stuff's not selling. Yet they don't make any effort to get people to come in to buy their stuff."

"Don't they know it's like a co-op?"

"Most of them do. They still come in every day hoping that something sold and that I have some money for them, so I know they are suffering too. Then, they linger in the shop all day and tell me about all their other problems. I got my own problems!"

"I'm sorry. Maybe business will pick up."

"Maybe. Folks just aren't buying. I get it. They don't have extra money. It's the economy. People are losing their jobs. Cost of living is going up. You know how it is. I just don't see things getting better. I've always put the shop first. I've always lived in the moment, but I think I need to start thinking about myself and what the future holds."

"I know what might help," Seraphina said.

She took a business card out of her wallet and handed it to Zoë.

"What's this?"

"It's for a masseuse I run errands for sometimes. If I refer clients, I get a free massage. I've got a couple on the books so I'm going to ask him to give one to you."

"No, don't do that."

"I won't take no for an answer. You need to relax. This will help."

"I've never had a professional massage before," Zoë said.

"Really? You'll love Jaquan. He has strong hands," Seraphina said.

"Is he single?" Zoë asked.

"Girl! He gay!"

Chapter 7

With the rent paid up for the shop, and a couple of past due bills at home caught up thanks to her mom, Zoë made coffee and spent the morning making a grocery list. She was going to make spaghetti tonight; she had not made it in months. She was also going to buy a bottle of wine, maybe two. She'd been open for three hours and was absorbed in her list-making before the bell on the door rang.

"Hi there! Welcome to Hands—."

"How much for those zinnias?" a woman interjected, pointing to the flower pot on the counter. She had on large sunglasses and a red shiny raincoat, even though it wasn't raining outside.

"Oh, these aren't for sale."

"Fifty dollars!"

"For these?"

"Yes!" the woman said, digging frantically in her purse.

"This is an art shop," Zoë said, not really sure what to say.

"Fine," the woman said, looking around. "How much for that?"

"What?"

"That?" the woman said pointing to a large oil and wax painting hanging on the wall. It was a vibrant, abstract piece of the Mississippi River and the downtown cityscape.

"The artist wants six hundred," Zoë said.

"Fine. I'll take that and the flowers. Cash okay?"

"Sure."

Zoë couldn't believe it. It was the most money she'd made in a single day all year.

"Why the zinnias?" Zoë said, hoping not to offend her or sound intrusive.

The woman let out a small sigh as if Zoë was a child asking twenty questions. She stopped digging in her pocketbook and lowered her glasses to look at Zoë.

"There's a woman, Martha, in our office who is retiring today. Good riddance! I never liked Martha. But she's allergic to any flower that has a scent, and the flower market on Union couldn't help. 'Why do we have to get her flowers at all?' I asked. Why? Because Cindy thought a gift card was too generic."

"Why not a cake?"

"Are you joking? She's diabetic."

"A potluck is nice."

"Too many food allergies in the office, and cheapskates."

"One of those large greeting cards for everyone to sign?"

"That's what Cindy said," the woman scoffed as if she was offended that Zoë had agreed with Cindy.

"If you don't like Martha, why not just get scented flowers and say you forgot?"

"I'm not a monster! Plus, that's too obvious."

The woman counted the money again and then handed it to Zoë. Zoë saw the six one hundred dollars and the fifty fanned out in her hand so she didn't bother counting it again.

"Why the painting?"

"That's for my fiancé, Richard."

"Does he like art?"

"No, but I do. It will look perfect in our dining room. You know, you really should sell flowers in here."

"This is an art shop," Zoë repeated.

"So what? I saw those flowers through the window as I was walking by and they are the only reason I came in. The flower market on Union doesn't have anything as nice as these. Where'd you get them?"

"My mom grew them."

"Well, your mom is a superb gardener. You can tell her I said that. Is this a dildo?" the woman asked, pointing to the same vase that Alexandra had asked about.

"It's a vase."

"Perfect! Here. Put the flowers in it," she said handing the vase to Zoë.

"You don't think Martha will be offended?"

"I'm counting on it!"

Zoë took the flowers in the back and attempted to repot them as best she could. She knew nothing about flowers, but they did look good in the dildo vase.

"How much do I owe you for the vase?"

"The artist has fifty dollars on it, but since you bought the painting and the flowers I'll give it to you for half price."

"Are you kidding me? I took up money in the office for this bitch. I intend to spend every penny of it."

"Okay, how much do you have left?"

"Here," she said, handing Zoë another hundred dollar bill.

"Need change?" Zoë asked.

"Nope!"

"Thanks. That's very kind of you."

"I mean what I said about the flowers. Look at all these pots and vases you've got in here. Fill them up! You could put the flower market out of business," the woman said.

Zoë took the painting off the wall and helped the woman out to her car, a tiny red Mini Cooper convertible that matched her raincoat. Zoë thanked her again and waved as the woman sped away.

She went back into the shop and noticed how drab it seemed without her Mom's zinnias. Maybe the woman was right. She picked up the phone and called her Mom.

"Ma, do you have any more zinnias?"

"Does Frampton start drinking before noon?"

"I take it that's a yes."

"Why do you ask?"

"Can I buy some?"

"Buy some flowers? You don't have any money."

"I have some left."

"Some of my casino winnings?"

"Yes."

"So you want to pay me *my* money for *my* flowers?"

"Yes."

"Keep the money. If you will come over and pick them, you can have all the flowers you want."

"What's the catch?"

"Go to the casino with me again Friday morning."

"Does it have to be at 3am?"

"Yes."

"Okay."

"And help me plan Frampton's birthday party next month."

"Anything else?"

"And come to the party."

"Damn it."

She hung up with her mother and called her friend, Matthew.

Chapter 8

Zoë had known Matthew since he first moved to the city almost twenty years ago. He'd even worked in her shop for a few years. Matthew ran his own shop now. It was called One Man's Trash and he sold refurbished furniture.

He'd been working in an old warehouse space downtown, but he was getting ready to open a proper storefront at the new Crosstown Concourse. It was in the old Sears Warehouse building, a giant castle-like structure overlooking Midtown that had stood vacant for almost two decades. It was being renovated and turned into apartments, shops, restaurants, and meeting places. Its grand opening was just a few months away.

Matthew had become a very talented carpenter over the years and had accumulated a workshop full of tools and equipment. Each morning before the city woke up, Matthew got in his truck and drove through the neighborhoods all over town and picked up pieces of furniture off the curb that people had trashed. Broken chairs, step ladders, sofas, book shelves, headboards, and end tables were all treasure, and they didn't cost him anything. In his spare time, he made pottery that Zoë displayed and sold in her shop.

"You're so butch," Zoë always told him when she'd see him in his faded denim jeans, dirty boots, and flannel shirts.

"Butch? Are you calling me a lesbian?"

"Would you prefer I call you daddy?"

"Just don't call me a bear. I hate that."

"Grrrr," Zoë teased.

Matthew had definitely grown up and filled out. He buzzed his hair now and even had a short beard that had just begun to show a hint of gray in his sideburns and on his chin. His arms were solid and burned red from the sun. A silver chain that Zoë had given him for his thirtieth birthday twinkled around his neck, nestled in the chest hair that he still trimmed. He kept his shirt unbuttoned and loose at the neck; his shirts were usually missing a few buttons anyway.

Matthew was no longer the small town, baby faced club

kid who had searched for love on the dancefloor. Recreational drugs and cocktails turned into beer and whiskey, and the search for love turned from long-term to temporary. Thanks to hook-up apps on cell phones, Matthew was rarely without a companion, usually ones that were half his age and always impermanent.

He'd experienced love once or twice early on, but now he was in love with other things. Creative things. Those things never cheated on him. They never hurt him or lied to him. They were always there for him, and he loved those things for that.

"Hello," Matthew whispered, answering the phone in a heavy gruff.

"Don't tell me you were asleep," Zoë said.

"Not anymore."

"You alone?"

"Yes."

"You lying?"

"No. He just left."

"Let me guess. Chadd with two D's?"

"Nah. Marc with a C."

"Ooh! I love Marc with a C. How's he doing?"

"You've never met him. He's Brian's ex. Remember Brian?"

"Brian with an I or Bryan with a Y?" Zoë asked, purposely

being facetious.

"Brian with an I. Bryan with a Y moved to Atlanta."

"How's Brian doing?"

"Which one?"

"You keep in contact with both of them?"

"Of course. Bryan with a Y invited me to come visit him in Atlanta sometime. And Brian with an I was here last night too."

"Seriously? I thought you said him and Marc broke up."

"They did. That doesn't mean we can't all be…friends."

"I sold your dildo vase," Zoë said, quickly changing the subject.

"Finally! Who bought it?"

"It was some stuffy lady in a red rain coat with a matching convertible. She was going to give it to a coworker as a retirement gift."

"Ha! She must not like her coworker very much."

"She also paid me for some flowers to put in it."

"Flowers? Where'd you get those?"

"They were some zinnias in a pot that Zandy had brought in for me. The woman saw them and wanted them. She gave me fifty bucks for them, then she bought your vase, and she bought a painting too. She said I should sell more flowers."

"But there's a flower market on Union."

"She'd gone there already. Apparently, they didn't have

zinnias or at least ones she liked."

"You thinking about doing it?"

"Maybe."

"Do you think it will piss off the artists?"

"Maybe some, but they'll get over it. Especially if some of their shit starts selling."

"Where are you going to get the flowers?"

"Ma's got a garden full of them. She said I could have all I want if I'll pick them."

"Let me guess. You want me to help?"

"Well…yes. But that's not the only reason I called you. I also need more vases and pots," Zoë said.

"Dildo vases?"

"I'll take all of it, whatever you got."

"That's what Marc said."

Chapter 9

"You need this?" Zandy asked after breakfast as she settled the check and counted her winnings.

It was 4am and they had planned on leaving right after they finished eating. It'd been a slow night at the casino. Zandy had not even cleared a thousand, but she knew when to walk away. She handed half across the table to Zoë.

"Nah, I'm good," Zoë said.

"My daughter turning down money? Hmpf."

"Well, you are giving me your flowers."

"Yeah, about that, what do you intend to do with my flowers?"

"Sell them."

Zoë told her mom about the spastic woman who insisted on buying the zinnias.

"I wanted that vase!" Alexandra said.

"You did not."

"You're right. It was hideous!"

"Hey now! Matthew made that vase."

"Don't tell him I said that."

"He's going to come over and help me pick the flowers."

"Who's he doing these days? I mean…*how's* he doing?"

"He's doing, that's for sure."

"Why aren't you?"

"Ma, you know Matthew is gay."

"That's not what I meant."

"I am getting a massage tomorrow. Seraphina is treating me," Zoë said, trying to change the subject. She hated discussing her love life, though non-existent, with her mother.

"A massage with a happy ending?" Zandy teased.

"Nope. Her masseuse is gay too."

"Do you even know any straight men?"

"You know I live in Midtown!"

Midtown was the gay mecca of Memphis.

"You need to move to Southaven or some area where the straight men are."

"Straight men like Frampton?"

"Frampton is from Orange Mound."

"Seraphina met a guy at Time Out the other night and took him home."

"Why aren't we going to Time Out with Seraphina then?"

"They don't have slot machines."

"So you think this whole flower thing will work?"

"It's worth a shot."

"Look at my daughter! Taking a gamble on things."

"I learned from the best, didn't I?"

"Damn right."

Zoë fell asleep in the car on the drive home, like always. She dreamt of getting a massage with Matthew in a field of zinnias.

Chapter 10

"Welcome to Urban Oasis," the young sexy girl behind the desk said when Zoë walked in.

She was a bit too sexy, and for a moment she made Zoë wonder what type of massage parlor this was. The girl had long, perfect braids. Her manicure was immaculate, as was her make-up. She wore a cute, tight track suit that showed off her ample cleavage.

"I have an appointment with Jaquan."

"Name?"

The girl sounded judgmental, or maybe it was just Zoë. She was a bit nervous.

"Zoë."

"Oh! You're Seraphina's friend," the girl's snobbish demeanor immediately changed.

"Yes, I am."

"Jaquan is double-booked, but Kyson is going to take care of you."

"Who?"

"Kyson. He just started a few weeks ago, but he's professionally trained and has been a massage therapist for eight years. He'll take good care of you."

Zoë took out her cell phone and sent a quick text to Seraphina:

Girl, what was the name of that guy you took home from Time Out?

Kyson. Why?

Just got to Urban Oasis. Jaquan overbooked. My masseuse is named Kyson.

Wha??? Can't be him.

Receptionist said he just started.

Have you seen him yet?

No. How will I know if it's him?

Girl, you'll just know. Keep me posted. Ooh…Take a photo!!!

How am I going to do that?

Figure it out!!

I'll try. TTYL.

Enjoy!

"Zoë, this is Kyson."

"Hi, Zoë. Ready for your massage?"

Zoë looked up from her phone and the sexiest man ever was standing before her. He looked exactly like the guy Seraphina had described, right down to that muscled chest. His tight shirt left little to the imagination. What a waste of cloth! Zoë wanted to be that shirt right now.

She hoped he wasn't wearing a cheetah print thong, because it was all she could see as she fantasized about what he might look like nude from the waist down.

Seraphina was right. It had to be him.

Chapter 11

Matthew usually preferred looking for discarded furniture on his own. He'd grab a coffee and a breakfast sandwich from the convenience store around 5am, and then drive around before the morning rush hour kicked in.

He liked seeing parts of the city where he'd never been before, where people lived down suburban streets in quaint bungalows, where children felt safe enough to leave their bikes on the lawn overnight, where flower beds were mulched and weeded, and old pieces of furniture were left on the sidewalks with the trash. It was always out with the old and in with the new in these neighborhoods. Families were always buying stuff.

Lately there had been some larger pieces he couldn't lift on his own. He scored a credenza and a chiffarobe last week on Claybrook but had to pay a trash collector to help him load them in the truck. He knew all the trash guys and their schedules and followed them around like kids chasing the ice cream truck. Some of them would text him photos if they thought there was something he'd like. They'd leave it on the sidewalk for him and even tell him what street it was on.

When Marc offered to ride along with him, Matthew wasn't so sure he wanted the company but he knew he could use the muscle. As usual, they'd met at the Pipeline for happy hour the night before.

Pipeline was a hole-in-the-wall leather bar. It was a long way off from The Red Square, a popular dance club that Matthew frequented back in the day when he first moved to Memphis. It had only stayed open for a year or two before changing owners and changing names half a dozen times like all the other gay bars in town. With every new coat of paint, a new clique called it home before aging out or moving on.

But not Pipeline.

It had stayed the same for years. Matthew would have cringed at the place back when he was what the mature crowd called a "puppy," those smooth chested baby-faced twinks and gym rats in tight pants and designer tanks. Now, Matthew fit right in with the older guys when it came to playing pool and drinking beer, but at the end of the night his sexual appetite was always satisfied by gym rats over daddy bears.

After Matthew left his downtown warehouse space for the day, he'd texted Marc who was already at the bar waiting for him. Matthew was looking forward to moving One Man's Trash into its new space soon. Crosstown Concourse was less than a mile from his house, and even closer to the bar so walking between home, work, and his favorite watering hole would never be a problem.

Marc had one too many Long Islands at the bar and wanted Matthew to take him home, and by home he meant back to Matthew's place. Matthew had yet to have a romp with Marc without Brian present so he was up for it.

"You sure Brian won't be jealous?" Matthew said.

"No, silly. You know we aren't together anymore."

What did Matthew care? Marc was the hotter one of the two anyway, despite the prickly chest which he insisted on keeping trimmed a bit too close. At least he was good in bed. Definitely what Zoë would have labeled "freaky."

"What are you going to do with all this stuff?" Marc said once the truck was so full they had to call it quits.

He'd been quiet most of the morning, and Matthew knew his head was throbbing from all the drinks and from having to get up so early. He knew Marc wouldn't volunteer to do this again.

They'd scored some wicker furniture pieces, a couple of end tables, a desk, a book shelf, some kind of old garden potting table, and even a couple of lamps.

"I told you I refurbish it and sell it."

"Do you ever wonder if you end up selling a piece back to someone who originally threw it out?"

"Ha! I never thought about that."

They unloaded the truck and Matthew showed Marc the inside of his warehouse space. Marc admired an old birthing chair that Matthew had turned into a coffee table. He wanted to buy it, but Matthew let him have it instead as compensation for helping him.

"I love this warehouse. It's so industrial," Marc said, looking up at the ceiling and its surrounding metal rafters.

"Prince Mongo used to throw raves here," Matthew said.

"No way! Is he still alive?"

"I don't know. If he is, he probably went back to his home planet of Zambodia."

Mongo was a local wealthy eccentric who had owned a couple of clubs that were popular for under-age drinking. He'd also run for mayor one year and come in fourth out of six candidates.

"Are you going to miss it?"

"Not really. I think business will pick up for me at Crosstown, plus it's closer to my house."

"And right across the street from the bar!"

"Yep, so do I owe you anything else for helping me today or is the table enough? Want this chair too?" Matthew said pointing to a side chair with metal legs.

"Hmmm, maybe. Sit down in the chair and let me look at you."

Matthew sat down in the chair and held his arms up in the air like a game show model, "How does it look?"

"I don't think I want the chair, but I know what I do want."

"What's that?"

Marc pushed Matthew's legs apart before kneeling down on the floor. Matthew leaned his head back. If this was how he had to pay Marc for the day, he'd definitely let him help again.

Chapter 12

"You can undress to your comfort level. Put your things on this chair. Lay on the table facing this direction, cover your waist with this towel, and your head goes here. I'll be back in five minutes, okay?" Kyson told Zoë.

"Thanks," Zoë said.

They'd gone into a small, dimly lit room with a large massage table in the middle. Saree fabric decorated the walls. The room smelled of eucalyptus. Kyson lit some candles on a side table and turned on a CD player. Soft harp music and chimes filled the air. Zoë would have preferred some Barry White. She texted Seraphina:

Girl, do I get naked?

I always do.

Of course she did!

What the heck! She was going to be face down and covered with a towel anyway. She got completely undressed and laid down. She adjusted the towel and put her face in the headrest which was lined with face cloths that smelled like tea tree oil. She took some deep breaths, closed her eyes, and tried to relax. Soon, there was a peck at the door and Kyson came back in.

"All set?"

"Mmmhmm."

"Any problem areas you'd like me to focus on?"

"All over."

"You got it. I'm going to use a mix of deep tissue and Swedish massage techniques. Just let me know if anything hurts and I'll adjust my pressure."

"Okay."

"You like the music?"

"Not really."

Kyson laughed.

"How about this? It's Enya."

Zoë preferred Yanni but she wasn't about to admit that now. She just wanted to get the massage started so she could start envisioning herself in titillating scenarios with Kyson while he was rubbing her back.

"I'd like to see what's in ya..." Zoë whispered under her breath.

"What's that?"

"Oh nothing! Enya's fine."

"So this is your first professional massage?"

"Mmmhmm."

"Great! Don't worry. Just relax. I'll take good care of you."

With her face down in the headrest she could hear him moving around the room behind her and prepping things. She turned her head to the side for a quick peek and caught herself looking right at his perfectly round bubble butt. He was bent over getting a bottle of oil out of the cabinet. She quickly turned her head back before he saw her.

"You're very tense," he said, as he lay his hands on her shoulders and began to rub oil down her back. "Try to relax and let go."

"Mmmhmm—."

She tried not to moan, at least not out loud. It didn't take long for her to "let go" once he started kneading. The tension in her muscles lifted. She was glad he didn't try to talk to her or ask silly questions like they do at the dentist's office. She couldn't even focus on the music as her mind wondered elsewhere.

The massage was an hour of pure pleasure. When it was over, she had not felt this relaxed since she smoked pot on the patio when she'd go clubbing with Matthew back in the day. She almost fell asleep several times, but she was afraid she'd snore or that some random vision would pop into her head and ruin her day dream fantasies of Kyson.

Seraphina had told her it was customary to leave a bigger tip since the massage was free. She didn't mind; Kyson had earned it though it did make her feel like she was paying a hustler when she handed him the three twenties.

She wondered if he felt like a cheap hustler? Or maybe he was a hustler and did other things besides massages? Her mom had asked about a happy ending. What did she know about that?

After she'd dressed and was ready to leave, Kyson checked in with her to ask how she felt.

"I feel great. Thank you so much," she said.

What she really wanted to say was horny.

He gave her his business card which had a headshot of him on it. She was glad because she was still thinking about how she was going to snap a pic of him for Seraphina. Now she didn't have to.

Chapter 13

Seraphina was at the jewelers when she got Zoë's text from Urban Oasis. She was picking out a diamond necklace for Alastair Phinster, a wealthy client of hers, to give to his wife for her birthday.

"Would you like to try it on, Seraphina?" Jake, the salesman, asked. She went to Jake for all of her jewelry needs.

"Of course, darling."

She turned around and held up her hair so that he could fasten the necklace around her neck. When she turned back around to face him, he already had the mirror in hand and was holding it up for her.

"Beautiful! Who's the lucky lady?" Jake asked.

"Colette Phinster."

"That's Phinster with a P. H!" Jake said, with his hand on his hip, imitating the old bag.

"So acidic!" Seraphina said.

Jake laughed. No one else ever got that joke.

"What floozy did Alastair get caught with now?"

"I think this is a birthday gift."

"I know a guy from the gay men's chorus who said Alastair used to frequent the dark room at Amnesia back in the day. Apparently, his nickname was Alastair *Sphincter* then. I bet you can guess why!"

"He pays me in cash, so I don't care who he sleeps with."

"How long have you been working for him?"

"Since right after the floozy that died in their house. Remember when that happened?"

"Yes! I remember reading about that in the papers. The girl's name was Charity. Reckon she was giving it away?"

"Ha! No. Alastair is hideous. I doubt even Colette ever sleeps with him without getting paid first."

"Rumor was Colette walked in on them in bed together, and she pushed Charity down the stairs."

"I believe that."

"Have you ever met her?"

"Oh yes! I work for her too."

"Doing what?"

"Planning cocktail parties mostly. I also hired all of her pool boys."

"How many does she have?"

"Just one."

"Is he hot?"

"Why do you think she got me to hire him?"

"Girl! How many has she gone through?"

"Four or five at least. She doesn't sleep with them. She just gets tired of looking at the same one all the time."

"Don't we all? Do any of her second-hand pool boys need jobs?"

"Jake, do you even have a pool?"

"No, but that's not the type of job I had in mind."

Jake took the necklace off for her. While he boxed and wrapped it for her, she checked her texts again:

Kyson was A-MA-ZING!

Happy ending? LOL

I wish! I did get happy looking at his end.

It was like gripping a couple of brioche buns.

I wanna bite those buns, hun.

Massage helped?

Yes! TY.

Did you take a pic?

Even better. Got his business card. It has his pic on it.

Show me!

Zoë sent a pic of her holding the business card up next to her mouth. She was sticking her tongue out and attempting to lick Kyson's face. Seraphina texted back:

That's him!

He's mine now.

We can share.

You've got Jaquan.

Still think Kyson is gay?

Bi maybe? I'm so relaxed I can't think. You should ask Jaquan!

Good idea!

Chapter 14

"Thanks for helping and for letting me use your truck. Want some gas money?" Zoë asked Matthew.

"Is Zandy making lunch?"

"Of course."

"We're even then. What's she making?"

"Fried chicken and potato salad."

"Yes! Does she still make the potato salad with Durkee's?"

"Is there any other way?"

Matthew had met her at the shop and brought all of his pots and vases with him. He'd tried ceramics and glass blowing through the years, but it was the clay pottery that he excelled at. He liked putting on some music and then just sitting at the potter's wheel and watching each piece take shape in his hands. He had two electric kilns for firing. He glazed and stained most pieces in solid colors until Zoë gave him a paint set for his birthday a few years ago.

"No dildo vases?" Zoë said.

"Look in the back seat."

"Yes! Yes! Yes!"

He'd brought about thirty pieces total, all various shapes and sizes including four new phallic vases.

"Only four?" Zoë asked.

"I only had two before you told me you sold the one you had. Those others are fresh out of the kiln."

"I like the way you made the paint drip down the sides."

"I call this one Derrick," Matthew said, holding one of the vases up for her to admire.

"Hmmm…was Derrick uncut?"

"No. Oh wait…this one is Derrick," Matthew said, putting the vase down and picking up the largest of the four vases.

"I like Derrick," Zoë said.

"So did I."

"I know just what to do with him! By the way, are you going to come to the open house?"

"When is it?"

"Sunday."

"I'll be there. Still want to do the riverboat cruise with me on Saturday to see the fireworks?"

"Yep as long as you teach me how to arrange flowers."

"Oh, you assume just because I'm gay that I know how to arrange flowers?"

"You do, don't you?"

"Of course!"

Chapter 15

Zandy's back yard had more flowers than the Memphis Botanical Garden. There were potted plants and sculptures all along the stone pathway that curved through the flower beds.

"Did you bring garden gloves?" she asked.

"Of course," said Matthew.

Zoë kept quiet.

"Zoë, I have a pair you can borrow."

"Thanks, Ma."

"Do you need floral shears?"

"Brought those too," Matthew said.

"Zoë?"

"I have an extra pair you can use. I brought buckets too,"

Matthew said.

"You came prepared," Zandy said.

"You *came* prepared," Zoë repeated, mocking her mom and teasing Matthew.

"You can cut all the zinnias you want. I've got marigolds too."

"How about those sunflowers?" Zoë asked, pointing to some bright yellow flowers nearby.

"Those are Black Eyed Susans," Matthew said.

Zoë rolled her eyes.

"The sunflowers are over there. You can take some of both if you want. How many pots do you plan to fill?" Zandy said.

"Fifty or sixty?" Zoë said, looking at Matthew.

"That sounds about right."

"I'll leave you to it. I'll call you when lunch is ready."

"You aren't going to help?" Zoë asked.

"You brought help. Besides, I'm giving you the flowers and feeding you lunch. Matthew, I made the potato salad just the way you like it."

"Thanks, Zandy."

They picked flowers for an hour and filled five buckets with stems before Zandy had called them in for lunch.

"Zandy, what makes your fried chicken so good?" Matthew asked.

"It's made with love, Baby."

"And lard," Zoë said under her breath.

"What did you say?" Zandy snapped.

"I said the Lord! Thank you, Lord!" Zoë said, choking up. She grabbed her glass of sweet tea and took a giant swig.

Matthew laughed and shook his head. He loved being around these two women when they were together.

"You should take me to the casino with you sometime," Matthew said.

"You'd have to get up early," Zandy said.

"Ma, he doesn't usually go to bed until that time. He can handle an all-nighter."

"What time do you go?"

"3am," Zoë said.

"Why so early?"

Zandy held up her hand and rubbed her fingers together indicating money.

"I'm in. Let's do it," Matthew said.

"After the open house," Zoë said.

"What do you think of this whole flower thing she's planning?" Zandy asked Matthew.

"I think it's a good idea. It's worth a shot. Doesn't hurt to try something new," Matthew said.

"Plus, we've already picked all these flowers," Zoë said.

"I can't supply you all year. What are you going to do then?"

"Seraphina's working her magic. She knows a couple of florists who might be able to hook me up with a wholesaler. We'll see what happens at the open house."

"What about containers? Do you have enough of those pottery pieces?"

"That's Matthew's department. He makes all of them."

"We won't run out," Matthew said.

"And if we do, I've got some other artists who do glasswork and ceramics. I'll never have a shortage of things to put the flowers in."

"Speaking of pottery, Zandy, we brought something to thank you for lunch," Matthew said.

"For me?" Zandy said, fluttering her eyes and clutching her chest.

Matthew went out to the truck and came back with a large gift bag. He handed it to Zoë to give to her. Zoë put her hand to her mouth, trying not to laugh.

"What is it?" Zandy said, taking the bag from Zoë.

She moved the tissue paper back and looked inside and then looked up at Matthew and Zoë who were both laughing.

"And what do you call this?" Zandy asked, taking the vase out of the bag.

"Derrick!" they said in unison.

Chapter 16

Zoë had flyers professionally designed and printed for the open house. They had "Hands Across The Board Presents: Efflorescent" printed across the top.

"I think they misspelled something," Seraphina said.

"No they did not."

"F-flor-scent?" Seraphina said, trying to pronounce it.

"You're close. It's Ef-flor-es-ent."

"What does it mean?"

"It means a lot of things pertaining to flowers. Budding, blooming, blossoming. But it also means emerging, developing, rising. I thought that was a good metaphor for the shop."

"Okay. I like it."

Seraphina took a stack of the flyers to give to all of her clients and to leave around town while doing her errands.

"Efflorescent? Nice!" Matthew said.

"Thanks, Boo. Glad someone can say it correctly."

"What's wrong?"

"Seraphina couldn't pronounce it."

"It's perfect."

"Do you think people from Pipeline might come?"

"Are you joking? Queens love flowers."

"And dildo vases?"

"All you need is a Statue of David replica, a disco ball, and a bar and you could have a good old fashion tea dance."

Matthew took some of the flyers to put in One Man's Trash to give to his own customers and he also put a stack at the bar.

"Is there going to be a drag show?" one of his bar friends asked, reading the flyer.

"Come and find out."

"Are you performing?" asked another.

"Nah, it would take a lawn mower to shave my legs."

"I know a good *weed wacker* if you need one," his friend said, wiggling his eye brows.

Matthew gave him a wink.

"We do need someone to tend bar. You interested?"

"Can I leave my nipple rings in?"

"Yes, but it's not that type of event so wear a shirt."

"Cash bar?"

"Yeah."

"Tip pool?"

"Nope. All yours."

"Okay, I'll do it."

The night before the open house, Matthew helped Zoë set up the shop. He showed her how to measure the flower stems for each vase and to cut away excess leaves. They put plant food in the bottom of each pot and filled them halfway with water before putting the flowers in.

Matthew had brought some plant stands and side tables in for more surface space for all of the pots. Seraphina showed up with some take-out for everyone and then helped Zoë clean and dust. Soon, Hands Across The Board was filled with vibrant summer colors of red, yellow, and orange.

"Wow! This place looks great!" Matthew said.

"It really does." said Zoë.

The day of the event Zoë and Matthew made a trip to Sam's for alcohol, food, napkins, and utensils. It didn't take long to set up the bar and a table filled with trays of finger foods. Matthew rushed home to shower and change clothes. Zoë brought clothes and make-up to get ready at the shop. She closed the shop at 3pm to give herself an hour before the open house.

"Did you invite Kyson?" Zoë asked Seraphina, who was painting Zoë's nails.

"Yes, and Jaquan too," Seraphina said.

"Did you ask Jaquan about him?"

"I did. He said he doesn't think he's gay."

"What? Jaquan is gay! Doesn't he have gaydar? How is it I'm straight *and* a woman, and I thought he was gay?"

"You think everyone is gay."

Chapter 17

With just ten minutes to go and a line already forming outside the door, Zoë let Matthew in through the back door. Everything was perfect but Zoë was still running around checking on things.

"Do you think we need more ice? Do the flowers need more water? Let's empty this trash can. Turn the music on. Should I dim the lights when it gets dark? Where did we put the extra napkins?"

"Zoë, it's going to be okay. Everything looks great. The bartender is all set. He'll let me know if he needs anything. Seraphina and I will mingle and be your salesmen. We'll also restock the food table. You run the cash register."

"I'm just nervous."

"I know, but there's about twenty or thirty people already waiting to come inside. Everything will be fine."

"Let's open those doors then and get the party started!" Zoë yelled with excitement.

Seraphina opened the doors and greeted the crowd as they trickled in. The gays headed right to the bar. Matthew saw some of his regular customers and said hello to them. Seraphina immediately saw a few of her clients as well. Several artists with work on display had been invited to come and greet people and try to sell their work if they wanted.

It didn't take long before Zoë had a line waiting to check out with their purchases. Customers were buying two and three pots of flowers, along with art pieces, paintings, and jewelry too.

Zoë couldn't remember the last time the shop had been this busy, or this full with people. It reminded her why she'd opened the shop in the first place. This was what it was all about, bringing artists and art lovers together to share their passions. Who knew it only took flowers to do it?

"Jaquan!" Seraphina yelled when she saw him walking in the door.

Zoë heard her and looked up to see if Kyson had come with him. Sure enough, they were standing there together. Kyson had a big grin on his face and raised his eyebrows when he saw Seraphina. Maybe he was surprised that she knew Jaquan. Zoë thought Jaquan and Kyson looked like a couple. They were even dressed the same in black leather biker jackets.

"Hey Kyson!" some queen yelled from the bar.

Seraphina turned to see who had called out to him. Zoë heard them too and thought it must be obvious now.

"Pssst," Zoë said to get the guy's attention at the bar. "Do you know Kyson?"

"Of course."

"He gay?"

"Girl, why you asking?"

"Seriously."

"Well, I think he bats for both teams, if you know what I mean."

"I knew it!"

"Hey, Kyson and Jaquan! You guys going to Pipeline later?" Matthew said as he walked by.

"Of course!" said Jaquan.

"See you there. I'll be late. Gonna help Zoë clean up after this."

"Girl, did you hear that?" Seraphina whispered, running up to Zoë after excusing herself from Jaquan and Kyson.

"Yes, I did. Some guy over there told me he thinks Kyson is bi. Are you disappointed?"

"Not really. His impeccable pecs should have been a sign."

"Three words: Cheetah! Print! Thong! I told you."

"You were right."

"He swings both ways though, so you aren't out of the game."

"Yeah, but I don't want no man possibly leaving me *for* a man! Besides, now I think him and Jaquan are together. Jaquan probably just didn't want to tell me."

"Do you think Jaquan knows? Kyson could leave him for a girl," Zoë said.

"Oh! He gonna know cause I'm gonna tell him!"

"Ooooh, girl! You stirring trouble."

"Serves him right. You gonna get another massage from Kyson?"

"Uh, yeah!"

"You know you can look but you can't touch."

"I can dream about touching, can't I?"

"Hey! You wanna go dancing at Time Out with me tonight after this is over?"

"Yes, we've got reasons to celebrate!"

"We do?"

"Yes! Look at this crowd!"

"I know! You are selling out. People love the flowers."

"And both of us can stop thinking about Kyson and find us some new men to take home," Zoë quipped.

"This time I'm looking for average good looking men. No perfectly chiseled bodies or smart dressers."

"And no thongs."

"Should we ask if they are wearing thongs before we let them buy us drinks?" Seraphina asked, laughing.

"Yes, but if he does have a thong on, the next one's mine!"

Chapter 18

By the time the evening was over and the last guest had said good-bye, there wasn't a single stem or piece of pottery left. The walls had bare spots from the hanging pieces that had been taken down and sold. The shelves were half empty. The event had been a huge success.

Zoë paid the artists who were still hanging around their cut. She tried to pay Matthew too but he refused to take it.

"Are you sure?" Zoë asked.

"Absolutely! Keep it. I wanted to help."

"Let me make it up to you somehow."

"You can buy me breakfast when we go to the casino."

"Deal."

"How'd you do?" Matthew asked his bartender friend.

"Cha-ching! Baby, drinks are on me tonight if you give me a ride to the bar."

"Let's go!"

Once things were cleaned up, Seraphina and Zoë said good-bye to Matthew and his friend as they headed to Pipeline. Zoë locked the door and thanked everyone again for everything they'd done for her as they walked to the parking lot.

"Say hi to Kyson for us," Seraphina said to Matthew sarcastically.

"Maybe I'll take Kyson home tonight," Matthew said.

"No you will not!" Zoë said.

"Just kidding! Don't worry. I'll call you tomorrow. Don't drink too much tonight. We've got the riverboat cruise tomorrow."

"The same goes for you, mister."

"If the bar is packed, I might not even go to bed."

"If the bar is packed, you'll definitely go to bed. You might not go to sleep, but you'll go to bed."

"You slut-shaming me, woman?"

"You can't shame the shameless," Seraphina said.

"Guilty!" said Matthew.

Chapter 19

There was a small line waiting to get in to Time Out, but once the doorman saw Seraphina he motioned for her to come up to the front. He unhooked the red velvet rope and let her and Zoë pass.

"Thanks, Baby," Seraphina said, touching the bouncer on the shoulder.

He didn't smile or even speak to her. He just gave a quick nod and closed the velvet rope behind them as they walked inside.

"You pay for that?" Zoë asked.

"Honey, he pays me."

"Oh?"

"I keep his wife and his side piece happy."

"How?"

"He gives me money. I take them shopping and to the spa."

"Together?"

"No! When one of them gets mad at him, he texts me. I conveniently text whichever one is mad that day and ask her if she wants to go to lunch. My treat. Of course, he covers everything. Then we go shopping or get mani-pedis or massages. She pours her heart out to me and then she's not angry anymore."

"So you get paid to lend an ear and be a best friend?"

"Yes, but they don't know that."

"What if they find out?"

"They won't."

"Do you tell him what they say?"

"Only if it might get him out of the doghouse."

"That must cost him a lot."

"He's not my richest client, but I wouldn't keep doing it if the pay wasn't good."

"Damn! How much does a bouncer make?"

"Honey, he ain't no bouncer. That man owns the club!"

"I feel sorry for the two women."

"Don't be sorry for them. He takes good care of both of them, and I'd totally be friends with them outside of work."

"I wanna be a kept woman someday," said Zoë.

"The wife or the side piece?"

"Depends on how much he's worth! And as long as you work for him, you'd tell me everything, right?"

"As long as he's paying for me to take you to lunch! C'mon, let's get a drink."

The Time Out Club was packed inside. Music was thumping and rattling the walls. A smoke machine had clouded the air over the dance floor. Colorful rays of light bounced off the clouds. Red and green lasers vibrated across the crowd. Six disco balls were spinning overhead.

They ordered drinks at the bar. Seraphina handed the bartender cash, but he put his hand up and indicated two men at the other end of the bar had covered them. Seraphina raised her glass to them to say thank you.

"Here we go," Seraphina said to Zoë.

"Are they cute?" she asked.

"Not bad. I could be wrong, but they look half our age."

"Come to Mama!"

The two women clinked their glasses together in a toast.

Chapter 20

It was too loud for proper introductions, but the two boys who'd paid for their drinks knew how to dance so Zoë and Seraphina let them bump and grind for a bit on the dancefloor. After several songs, the two women excused themselves to go to the restroom and to discuss what's next.

"So? What do you think?" Seraphina asked.

"I don't know about yours, but mine's got bad breath. Smells like someone is spilling spoiled milk down my neck."

"Mine's gripping my booty too tight. Probably be like riding a horse."

"I say we cut 'em loose."

The club was big enough to get lost in the crowd so that's

just what they did. They ordered another round of drinks and paid for themselves and then hit the dancefloor together.

"Girl, I'm getting tired. You ready?" Zoë said to Seraphina after a few songs.

"Already? We going home alone tonight?"

"You can sleep at my house if you want."

"You got some Baileys?"

"You know I do. And Kahlua."

"Nightcap at Zoë's!"

"Let's go."

At Zoë's place, she mixed them each a Baileys and Kahlua on ice, and they changed into their nightgowns. Seraphina always kept some night clothes and toiletries at Zoë's house for nights like these.

"So do you think you are going to continue with the flowers?" Seraphina asked.

"I don't know anything about flowers. I feel like a fraud selling them."

"You could learn. Take a class."

"They offer flower arranging classes?"

"I bet they do at the Botanical Garden or at the community center. Maybe even a college extracurricular course."

"I wonder how much that would cost?"

"You probably made enough tonight to cover it. I'll ask around and make some calls."

"This was fun. I'm just not even sure if I still want to sell art. I need to think about what comes next."

"You thinking of changing the shop up?"

"Maybe. Don't get me wrong. I love the shop. And I'll always love art, but I need to start making more money for myself."

"You could lower the commission you pay the artists."

"Nah, that's not fair to them. Wouldn't matter anyway. Sales have been so slow. I made more tonight than I've made all year. I need to find a way to supply my own product. Matthew giving me all of his pottery for the open house certainly helped."

"I can help too. Let me do some brainstorming and talk to some people."

They got into Zoë's bed and crawled under the covers. Zoë turned on a Netflix comedy. Both of them were asleep before the movie ended and before their glasses were empty.

Chapter 21

"Are you alone?" Matthew said. He'd waited and called Zoë later in the morning, giving her a chance to sleep in.

"No," Zoë whispered.

"Oh my God! You brought someone home with you?"

"Yes," she mumbled, trying to wake up.

"What's his name?"

"Seraphina."

"What?"

"Seraphina and I danced with some guys, but we came home together. How about you?"

"Homo alone."

"That's a first. Couldn't get Kyson and Jaquan's

attention?"

"I didn't try. I was calling to see if you want to go to brunch before the river cruise?"

"Sure, that sounds great."

"Pick you up at 11?"

"See you then."

She hung up the phone. Seraphina had already got out of bed and had just finished showering.

"Wanna go to brunch with me and Matthew?" Zoë asked.

"No, I've got some errands today," Seraphina said from the bathroom. She was standing in front of the mirror and putting on her make-up.

"Yours or a client's?"

"Both!"

"You should pay someone to do yours?"

"You wanna work for me?" Seraphina teased.

"You can't afford me, girl."

Midtown had a lot of great eateries and hotels that served brunch, but Matthew knew Zoë's favorite place was a little joint called The Beauty Shop. They had the best Bloody Marys and mimosas in town.

"Can I get you drinks?" the waiter said when they were seated.

"I'll just have coffee," Zoë told the waiter.

"No mimosa today?" Matthew asked.

"Not if I'm going to drink on the boat, and I'm definitely going to drink on the boat."

"You don't mind if I get started, do you?" Matthew asked. He told the waiter to bring him a Bloody Mary.

"Started? Do you ever end?" Zoë asked.

"I only had a couple of beer last night at the bar and then went home early, and I only had one drink at the open house. So were you happy with the turn out last night?"

"I was," Zoë said with a bit of a sigh.

"What's wrong?"

"I need to figure out if I'm going to try to do this whole flower thing or not, but I told Seraphina I'm not sure if I want to continue selling art too."

"The whole commission thing?"

"Yeah. I want to start making more money for myself. I've loved having the shop, but I just feel burnt out. I need something new. I thought the flowers would do it for me, but I'm still not sure. I don't know anything about flowers."

"You could learn. I could help you."

"That's what Seraphina said."

"So what next then?"

"I'm not sure. Give me some time to think about it."

Chapter 22

After brunch, Zoë asked Matthew to drop her off at the shop. Hands Across The Board was closed for the holiday, but she wanted to spend a few hours there alone before the sunset cruise. There was no real work to be done, nothing that couldn't wait until Monday, but she still wanted to be there.

"I'll swing back by and pick you up at 5, okay?" Matthew said.

"Sounds good."

She locked the door behind her and kept the lights turned off. She didn't want to risk having an artist stop by and want to come in. She needed some time all to herself to think.

She walked around the store admiring the empty spaces left

from the success of the open house. It felt good to see so much art finally sold, more than they'd ever sold before in one night. The post card spinning rack was half empty again. Even a few of the framed post-its had sold.

Tomorrow she would figure out how much she owed the other artists. They'd eagerly stop by throughout the week to get their money and probably bring new stuff with them to restock. The store would be full again by the end of the week.

Was it the flowers that had caused the success? Or the flyers? Or the word-of-mouth spread by Matthew and Seraphina who maybe begged people to come just to help Zoë out? They'd probably never own up to it, but she knew from the amount of people who they'd known that she owed a lot of the traffic to them.

Zandy told her she could only supply flowers for a few months at most. Those wouldn't cost her anything. But what would happen after that if she bought from a wholesaler? What kind of expense would that be on her? And how much of a loss would it be when the flowers weren't selling? The shop would look so depressing if she had to clean out dead flowers all the time.

If she put all of her attention on flowers, would the artists be mad at her? Would the art continue to sell? Would she have time to chat and counsel the artists who hung out all the time? She'd never admit it out loud, but that was the part she'd miss the least if she didn't have time to do it anymore.

She sat down at her desk and composed an email to send out to all of the artists who currently had pieces for sale. She let them know about the success of the open house. She told them she'd contact them individually to let them know if they had sold anything and how much they'd earned so they could arrange a time to stop by to get paid. Then, she told all of them *not* to bring new pieces to restock just yet. She wanted to get everyone paid and take inventory of the store first.

This would give her some time to decide what to do next. She hit send and then put on a Bob Marley record. She danced with herself a bit around the shop, savoring the time alone, before sitting down to read a book and wait for Matthew to return.

Chapter 23

"A bunch of gays on a riverboat? There's gotta be a joke in there I've missed," Zoë said to Matthew as they parked.

"Proud Mary!" Matthew said with a grin.

"There it is!"

"Our boat is called the Memphis Queen."

"This is going to be so much fun."

"Hey Matthew!" someone yelled from the boat.

Matthew looked up and saw Marc and Brian standing at the railing on the upper deck. He waved to them.

"Who's that?" Zoë asked.

"Marc and Brian."

"Bryan with a Y?"

"No, with an I."

"And Marc with a C?"

"You got it."

"Well, your threesome just became a fourgy. You're my date tonight!"

They boarded the giant steam boat at Beale Street Landing and found the nearest bar to get drinks. When everyone was aboard, the boat rolled up the river at a slow pace and stopped just beneath the Hernando de Soto Bridge which was lit up in red, white, and blue lights.

"It's beautiful, isn't it?" Matthew said.

"Yes, it is. I've seen it in paintings and photographs in the shop for years, but I never get tired of looking at it."

They clinked their beer bottles together in a toast just as the fireworks lit up the sky over the Mississippi Delta.

"I'm probably going to close the shop," Zoë said.

"Oh wow! Really?"

"Yeah, not just yet, but it's probably going to happen."

"What are you going to do?"

"I'm going to take a class or something. Try to learn about flowers. Maybe take a couple of business classes too so I can do this right."

"That sounds like a good idea."

"But I need a favor," Zoë said.

"Anything. You name it."

"Teach me how to make pottery."

"You going to put me out of business?" Matthew said, joking.

"Nah. I just want to learn how to do something with my hands. I want to make something. I want to make my own art."

"I get it. I've got an extra potter's wheel you can have."

"That would be great!"

Someone tapped Matthew on the shoulder from behind. He turned around to see Brian and Marc standing there. Matthew introduced both of them to Zoë. She tried not to smile or lead on that she knew of their tryst.

"Care if we swing by after the cruise?" Brian said to Matthew.

"Sorry. I've got plans after this with Zoë."

"No problem. Catch ya later. Nice meeting you, Zoë," Brian said as he and Marc walked away.

"You didn't have to do that for me. If you'd rather hang out with them, I understand."

"Nah. I want to hang out with you and create stuff."

Create.

She liked the sound of that.

Chapter 24

After the boat docked, Matthew and Zoë went back to his place. He set up the potter's wheel for her and showed her how to adjust the speed.

"Wow, that's a lot of clay," Zoë said when Matthew put a large mound of it on her wheel.

"Since this is your first time, it will be easier to work with a big piece."

"That's what *he* said," Zoë quipped.

They both laughed. Matthew put some clay on his wheel.

"Now let's get our hands wet," Matthew said, dipping his hands into the water bucket.

Zoë watched and mimicked him.

"Sit close to the wheel and keep your elbows close to your body. You'll want to push the clay forward once we get going."

Matthew sped up her wheel a bit for her.

"It'll be bumpy at first. Don't press against it too hard but hold it firm. As it spins, the clay will start to calm as it smooths itself out in your hands."

"How will I know?"

"It'll just feel right. You'll know from the touch. Don't be afraid of it. You can't mess it up."

Zoë cupped her hands around the clay as it spun. It felt slimy but she could feel the bumps slowly disappearing against her fingers.

"I feel like we should play Unchained Melody."

"Why?"

"It's from the movie, *Ghost*. Remember that scene with Sam and Molly?"

"I'm not as hot as Patrick Swayze was back then."

"I guess I look more like Whoopi than Demi."

"I'd much rather make pottery with you."

"*Matthew, you in danger, girl!*"

Zoë accidentally sped the wheel up. She tried to correct it and ended up denting the clay. It began to spin out of control and quickly lost its smooth shape. Matthew reached over and turned off the wheel.

"Don't laugh at me."

"You're doing fine."

"I'll call this piece Hot Mess," Zoë said.

"Nothing's wasted. Just roll it back into a ball like it was when you began and then you just start again."

"This is good therapy."

"Yes, it is."

She started again and kept control of the clay much better the second time. Matthew showed her how to press her thumbs on the top to start forming a cone. She copied him again, holding the side of her hand on top at an angle and pressing down. The tall cone of clay began to widen.

"Keep pressing down, but not too hard. Let the clay choose its shape."

"It's starting to look like a bowl!"

"Yes it is. Put your thumb on the edge and that will smooth the rim."

"How does it get the hole in the middle?"

"I'll show you. You can take your hands off yours for a minute and just watch me."

Zoë carefully lifted her hands from the spinning clay and then turned off her wheel. She watched as Matthew kept his left hand on the edge. He took his right index finger and pressed down in the middle, marking where the hole would start.

"Now, you just press down and pull out," he said.

She was amazed at how the piece seemed to open magically. It now looked like a perfect bowl. Once the opening was as wide as he wanted it, he moved his thumbs along the bottom and slowly scooped out extra clay. He used a wet sponge to moisten the clay, pressing down on the inside. He told her that keeps the inside from cracking.

"This is amazing!" Zoë said.

"It's fun. Isn't it?"

"I love it."

"Now you try."

He stopped his wheel so he could watch her. She started the wheel and wet her hands again. She cupped the clay and pressed her finger in the middle just like he did. Pulling her finger back, it opened and the bowl appeared. He handed her the sponge so she could finish the inside. Matthew showed her how to squeeze and lift the side to make the piece taller and skinnier.

"The hardest part is collaring the rim. You don't always have to do that."

"Are we done?"

"Almost. We just have to clear the extra clay off the bottom so that we don't have to trim a lot. Then we cut the piece with wire to remove it from the wheel. Wanna take a quick break first and have a drink? I want to show you something."

Matthew showed her some pottery shaped like human heads he'd been making. They had huge ears and fat noses to give them a comical look. The tops were open for flowers. He'd painted their eyes in a green or blue glaze and their hair in a dripping pattern of red or yellow glaze.

"I love these!" Zoë said.

"I call them pot heads. Thought the bright colors would look good with the zinnias or marigolds in them. I put a hole in the bottom for water to drain."

"Makes my little pot look like a kindergarten craft project."

"You gotta start somewhere. It took me months to be able to put handles on and make them look decent. That's why the ears on the potheads look so good. Don't worry. You'll get there."

"Thanks for showing me how to do all of this."

"Anything for you, Zoë."

After they'd finished their drinks, he showed her how to trim the excess clay and remove the piece from the wheel. They'd let it dry and then he would show her how to fire it later in the week.

He drove her home and waited until she was safe inside. The lights in her house flicked on and he saw her wave from the window, indicating she was safe inside and that he could drive on.

Zoë grabbed her laptop and crawled into bed. She went to YouTube and watched videos of people making pottery until she was tired and ready to sleep.

Matthew went to the bar.

Chapter 25

When he walked into Pipeline, several of his friends at the bar pretended to look at their watches, giving him a hard time about being late. He gave them the finger, laughed, and ordered a beer. Normally, on a Sunday night, he would have come in the early afternoon for happy hour.

"Brian said you were on the boat with a woman," one of his friends said.

"Yeah I was."

"You playing both sides now?"

"Maybe. What's it to you?"

"So you take her on a gay riverboat cruise?"

"No, silly! It was Zoë!"

"Ohhhh! How is she?"

"She's fine."

"She still got that art shop in Overton Square?"

"Yep, still there."

"Is she going to move?"

"I don't know. Why?"

"It was on the news last night. The owners are trying to sell that whole row of buildings. The neighborhood is worried whoever buys might tear them down. There's a group or something that's working on preventing that. She didn't mention it?"

"No, she didn't."

"Seems odd that the news would know before the tenants, but that doesn't surprise me."

"Thanks for telling me."

Matthew would call Zoë tomorrow to ask her about it. Maybe that was why she suddenly wanted to reinvent herself. Seemed odd for her not to mention it, but maybe she didn't want to talk about it.

He went out to the patio. It was a cramped closed-in spot on the back of the building with a raised deck that wrapped around a large oak like a treehouse. There was an area to sit underneath around the tree trunk and on the upper deck, a perfect spot for lewd things to be happening at this hour. You could always tell if something was happening because a crowd would be gathered on the deck if the bar was packed like it was tonight.

Matthew immediately spotted a crowd in the tree house. He could only see them from the waist up because of the wooden railings surrounding the deck, but he could tell several guys had their shirts off. Matthew could only imagine what was happening behind the railings. Guys always flocked up there like ants at a picnic. He was going to go up to the deck and join the fun when he felt a hand on his shoulder stopping him.

"There you are, sexy. Did you enjoy the cruise?" Marc asked.

"Yeah, it was nice. What about you?"

"Not really."

"Why not?"

"Well, the music was terrible and no dancing. The drinks were watered down. The bathrooms were disgusting. It felt like I was on a summer vacation boat trip at the lake with my parents."

Matthew thought to himself: *Typical gay male. Can't spend one night without a disco ball or the bass dropping out. I could never date this guy.*

"Well, it was for a good cause. All the money goes to the local Humanity House which helps gay teens."

"I'd rather just write a check. Besides, no one helped me when I was a teen and my parents kicked me out."

"Which is why you should be glad there's help now for others like you."

"Pfff…Who was that girl you were with anyway?" Marc sounded salty. He was definitely drunk.

"She's a friend. Her name is Zoë."

"That's right. She straight?"

"Yes."

"Ugh. There were several straight people on the boat. Can't get away from them!"

"It's nice to have friends and allies."

"Damn Breeders!" he squawked.

"Where's Brian?" Matthew asked, changing the subject. Marc was getting on his nerves, at least this side of him.

"He went home. Sea sick, I guess. What are you doing?" Marc said, reaching over and touching Matthew's shoulder.

"I'm going to finish my beer and then head home."

"Want some company?" Marc said, trying too hard to sound sexy.

"Not tonight. Thanks."

Marc immediately turned and walked away. Matthew let him go. He chugged his beer and then went back inside.

"Leaving already?" someone said behind him.

He didn't turn to see who it was. He just walked out the door and into the night, headed home.

It didn't matter how sexy someone was, or how nice of a

body they had, or even how good they were in bed. Matthew was immediately turned off by insolence or anyone displaying an attitude of rancor. It also didn't matter if they were drunk or not. People's true colors tend to show when they were.

Nothing had ever been serious with Marc. It had just been fun, but it was over.

Chapter 26

On Monday morning, Zoë went into the shop early. She knew artists would be eagerly stopping by to get paid. When she unlocked the door, the postcard photographer was the first one in the door, eager to restock his display.

"Didn't you get my email?"

"No, sorry."

"It's okay. Go ahead."

She let him restock. It would be better than a half-empty display sitting in the store. She paid him and he left right away before anyone else came in.

"Hi, Zoë!" someone else said, coming in just a few minutes later. Zoë had the feeling it was going to be like this all day.

It was Mindy. She made a lot of the jewelry in the case, necklaces and bracelets with small clay baubles or stones wrapped in copper wire hanging on simple black cords. Quite a few had sold at the open house.

"Hi, Mindy! How are you?"

"I'm good. I got your email. I hate to seem like I'm running in with my hand out, eager to get paid. I was actually in the area and thought I'd stop by. Sorry I couldn't make it to the open house."

"Girl, it's okay. I'm glad you sold some stuff. Happy to pay you."

"Do you need me to take what's left?"

"No. Why?"

"Well, you mentioned in your email about not restocking. I figured you were cleaning out the shop."

"I do want to clean. Maybe rearrange things a bit. But that's not why I sent that. I just wanted to take inventory first and get things in order before filling up the store again."

"Oh, I thought it might have been because of the news last night."

"News? What news?"

"No one's told you?"

"Told me what?"

"I just figured they sent letters to each business or something."

"Mindy! What news? Tell me!"

"They are going to try to sell this row of buildings. There was a whole thing about it on the news last night. The neighborhood is going to try to stop it. They're afraid the buildings will be torn down and turned into something depressing like a self-storage facility."

"What?"

"It's on the front page of the newspaper today too."

Zoë had brought the paper in and laid it on the counter but she had not had a chance to look at it. She grabbed the newspaper and unfolded it. The headline couldn't be missed: FRIENDS OF MIDTOWN ATTEMPT TO BLOCK SALE OF OVERTON SQUARE.

"No one told you?" Mindy said.

Zoë shook her head.

"Sorry."

"It's okay."

"Hey, while I'm here, would it be okay if I took the rest of my jewelry? I'm doing an arts and crafts fair next weekend and could use the inventory."

Zoë handed her the key to the jewelry case. Mindy took the rest of her stuff and left.

Mindy wasn't the only artist to stop in to get paid, and who mentioned the news that day. Others took what pieces they had not sold, giving some random excuse. There's no way they were all going to the same arts and crafts fair as Mindy. Zoë kept quiet and let them take their art. She couldn't blame them for being worried. It was perfect timing. If she wanted a sign of what she should do, this had to be it.

"Are you going to move to a new location?"

"Will you let me know what happens?"

"Are they going to tear the buildings down?"

"I heard it's going to be turned into a parking garage."

"You should move to Crosstown."

Everyone was full of questions and opinions, parading through the store to get their money and collect their art. No one asked how Zoë felt or what she herself was going to do. She was glad no one said anything. She'd spent a lot of time helping several of them to find answers to their own questions in life.

Now, for once, when she needed answers the most, she had none.

Chapter 27

"Girl, I've been texting you all day," Seraphina said to Zoë. She'd stopped in just as Zoë was locking up.

"Sorry, it's been a busy day."

"Good?"

"Not really. Just artists stopping in to get paid and take their stuff."

"Take their stuff?"

"Yep. You see the news?"

"Yeah, that's why I was texting you and why I came by."

"Please don't ask me what I'm going to do. If one more person asks me that today, I'm going to break," Zoë said. Her eyes grew watery.

"Oh, sweetie," Seraphina said, wrapping her arms around her and giving her a hug.

"It's just…everyone came in with their hands out, which is fine. They earned it and I emailed everyone and told them to come in. No big deal. But then everyone expected me to know what was going to happen next. I didn't even know about all of this until the first person who came in today told me."

"I'm so sorry."

"But instead of offering help, everyone started taking their pieces like they'd given up on the shop and were moving on. No one asked how I was feeling. It was all about the shop and where and when was I going to move and reopen."

"Well, you were in a quandary about what to do next. Maybe this is a sign?" Seraphina said.

"It's definitely a sign."

"Want to grab a bite to eat. My treat. We can talk about it if you want."

"Sure. Thanks."

They went next door to the Blue Note Café for soup and salad. Miss Beatrice Starr was standing in line when they walked in. She owned Starr Books which was on the other side of the café.

"Hi, Zoë," Beatrice said.

"Hi, Beatrice."

"Are you going to the meeting tonight?"

"What meeting?"

"Friends of Midtown is meeting tonight at The Cooper Young Grill to discuss our options."

"I didn't even know about the meeting."

"Didn't you get the announcement?"

"No."

"They taped announcements to our back doors this morning."

"I didn't use the back door today so that explains why I didn't get it."

Seraphina could tell Zoë was on edge. She was probably really close to telling Beatrice where to go.

"No, I'm not going," Zoë said.

"Why not?"

"Because right now I'm hungry and I want to eat dinner with my friend and then I'm going to go home and pour a glass of wine and take a bubble bath and try not to think about any of this."

"Must be nice."

"Yes, it will be nice. Thank you."

"Well, if they force us out I'm going to just close the bookstore and retire. The only reason I kept the shop open this long was to have an excuse to get out of the house and away from my husband. He died last year."

"Must be nice," Zoë repeated.

Beatrice looked appalled. Seraphina tried not to laugh. Zoë's demeanor never changed; she was trying desperately not to blow her lid. Beatrice turned back around and didn't say another word to them. She even changed her order to go.

"So, we don't have to talk about this now if you don't want to but I spoke to one of my clients who put me in touch with a local nursery who supplies wholesalers with flowers. They also teach flower arranging classes. Do you think you'd be interested?" Seraphina said.

"Yeah, I would. Matthew gave me a pottery lesson last night. I loved it. It felt good to make something of my own."

"That's the spirit. I'm sure someone today already said this, but you should think about moving to Crosstown. Maybe you and Matthew could be neighbors?"

"Yeah, actually someone did mention moving over there. I bet the rent is expensive though."

"Not as bad as you would think. The place is huge and there's lots of tenants lining up. They even have apartments for rent on the upper levels. It's going to be a melting pot of things. Just like Hands Across The Board has always been. Wouldn't you like to be a part of that?"

"I do like the sound of it."

Zoë wondered if Matthew might be interested in being a partner with her. They could share business expenses. She could run the sales floor and sell his pottery and furniture, which would give him more time to work on making things. She could do flowers, make some pottery too, and maybe even sell some art.

It sounded like a good plan. She just hoped Matthew would think the same thing. She didn't want to intrude on him or his space. If he wasn't into it, then maybe they could be neighbors like Seraphina suggested.

Zoë started thinking up cool names for a store. She needed to turn the page. Even if Matthew didn't want to go into business with her, if she decided to move her shop to Crosstown it deserved a new name. She was ready for a fresh start.

Chapter 28

The next morning was much better at the shop just because there were less artists coming in asking questions. As the news spread, a few called to check in and had questions about the future of Hands Across The Board. Zoë let every caller know she'd alert all the artists as soon as she knew more. Calls became so numerous she eventually stopped answering her phone. Several hours passed since she'd opened without a single person stopping by, customers or artists. It made her sad that another day of no sales was evident, but she did not mind the quiet. That changed when Beatrice popped in just before lunch time.

"Hi, Beatrice. How was last night's meeting?"

"You closing shop already?" Beatrice asked, ignoring Zoë's greeting as she sauntered up to the counter.

"No, why do you ask?"

"This place is half empty."

"We had an open house this past weekend and sold quite a bit."

"Must be nice."

"Yes, it was nice."

"I suppose you want to know how the meeting went since you didn't come?"

"Not really," Zoë said under her breath.

"What?"

"Sure! How did it go?"

"Seems the buildings are not up to code. It's cheaper for them to just tear them down and rebuild instead of fixing them."

"Not up to code?"

"Handicap access. Sprinkler systems. Restrooms. All that stuff."

"And it's cheaper to just tear down and start over?"

"Apparently so."

"That sounds wasteful."

"Yes, it does. Anyway, as I told you yesterday I'm going to call it quits and retire. Book sales are in the toilet anyway thanks to Ebooks and online discounts.”

“I'd probably do the same, Beatrice.”

“So you are closing up then?”

“I'm thinking about moving to Crosstown and starting something new.”

“Good idea! I think some of the other businesses around here will do the same. I know the record shop on the corner is moving over there.”

“Any word on what they are going to build here?”

“Not much was said. They are entertaining the idea of another shopping complex with all the stores on the inside. It certainly won't have the character all of the old buildings have now.”

“No it won't. I've always loved the way our stores look. It's part of the charm of Overton Square.”

“If they do build that, it will be across the street and be part of the new movie theater. So where we are standing now will probably be a parking garage.”

“I thought there was some historical society or something that wanted to save these buildings?” Zoë asked.

“They did, but someone would have to buy the property and the city would make them bring it up to code. A building inspector was at the meeting and told them how much it would cost, and that quickly changed their minds.”

“How much?”

"The property is going to sell for a couple of million. It would take a couple more to meet code."

"Wow! I guess Friends of Midtown don't have any rich friends, huh?"

"No they do not. One member asked for a second appraisal of the property, but he wants the city to pay for it. That's not going to happen. The city is on board for pushing forward, which means pushing us out."

"Leave it to the sardonic politics of the city to ruin everything!"

"Business is down in this area. You and I both know that. They think building something new will bring customers back."

"Ha! Maybe at first, but I bet half the shops in the new place stay empty! And they'll try to get some big name brand stores to commit to entice shoppers. They don't care about us."

"They offered a rent stipend to the existing shops if they'd commit to moving into the new complex."

"A rent stipend? Who's going to pay my rent, my bills, and buy my groceries while I wait for them to build it? I don't have any savings I can live on till then," Zoë said.

"And who's to say we could afford the rent in the new place?"

"Exactly!"

"Well, Beatrice, thanks for telling me. I'm sorry about yesterday at The Blue Note. I was not in a good mood because I'd just found out about all of this."

"No worries," Beatrice said, waving her hand away.

"It would have been nice had they sent a representative around to tell each of us personally or called a meeting just for the business owners."

"Are you kidding me? They were too afraid we'd turn into a mad mob or something."

"I probably would have spit in their eye."

"I would have liked to have seen that."

"I would have liked to have done it!"

Beatrice left. Zoë turned out the lights, locked the door and went home. Normally, she'd still been open for a few more hours, but there was no reason to stay open today. It would have been a waste of time since Beatrice was the only person who'd even come in today.

Zoë didn't want to be there; she needed the time away from this place to focus on some new thoughts and the days ahead.

Chapter 29

Seraphina booked a meeting for Zoë with the local grower and florist she'd mentioned. The name of the place was The Green Room. Seraphina gave her the business card of the man who owned the place. His name was Braden. The business card was shaped like a small leaf.

"He sounds hot. Have you met him?" Zoë asked.

"No. I usually deal with some of his employees. I did speak to him on the phone once. He has a sexy voice. He goes by Brad."

"As in Brad Pitt?"

"He sounds like he could be as sexy as Brad Pitt."

"Brad Pitt from *Thelma and Louise* or Brad Pitt from

Moneyball?"

"Brad Pitt from *Troy* maybe?"

"Even better!"

"If he has long blonde curls and is walking around shirtless, you better call me."

"Please don't let him be gay. Please don't let him be gay. Please don't let him be gay," Zoë chanted.

"What if he's married?" Seraphina asked.

"Please don't let him be gay. Please let him be single. Please don't let him be gay. Please let him be single."

Zoë dressed like she was going to a job interview. She even put on a little more makeup than usual and painted her nails. She didn't really have a reason other than it made her feel good, and maybe she was dressing to impress a certain man named Braden.

Why not?

She was turning the page and starting a new chapter in her life. She was learning new things. She felt good about this. Why not dress the part?

"Do you want me to go with you?" Seraphina asked.

"Nah, I'll be fine."

"Girl, you got this."

"I'm not even sure what *this* is, but I'm about to find out."

Chapter 30

Matthew had already picked his new space at Crosstown Concourse. He let the security guard know he was meeting the realtor today. The guard checked his clipboard and gave Matthew a VISITOR badge before letting him inside.

The massive concrete building and its parking structure that had loomed over Midtown like a Vampire's ancient castle was suddenly full of life inside. Construction workers and janitors were rushing about. Restaurants and café employees were setting up kitchens and painting walls. A stack of lime green chairs sat in the middle of the first floor lobby on a skid, still wrapped in plastic and waiting for their new home somewhere in the giant building.

Years ago, Matthew's truck had broken down near the old warehouse. He'd pushed the vehicle off the road and into its parking lot, which glistened with fragments of shattered glass. He'd noticed a broken window on the side of the building and peeked inside to a black cave filled with debris and darkness.

His new store was on the lower level near the loading dock which would be perfect for any of his customers buying large pieces. He was meeting with the realtor to sign the lease so the space would officially be his and he could begin moving in and setting up. The realtor had put a small desk and two chairs in the middle of what would become Matthew's new store.

"So this is it?" Matthew asked the realtor.

"This is it. Are you nervous?"

"Not nervous, but I am excited. Man, this place is huge."

"It's amazing. Isn't it?"

"I'm just glad they were able to reuse the existing structure instead of tearing it down."

"Me too. The renovation has been massive, but well worth it. We've got art space, meeting space, restaurants, shopping, fitness, and apartments too. These urban mixed-use developments are popping up everywhere in old buildings and dead shopping malls."

"I'm glad to be a part of it."

"We're glad you are here, Matthew. I'll see you at the opening ceremony?"

"Of course."

He signed the paperwork and they shook hands. The realtor stacked both chairs upside down on the small desk and rolled it out into the hallway. He gave Matthew a handbook, a map of the building, and a schedule of upcoming events leading up to opening day. Then, he handed Matthew the keys and left.

Matthew stood there in the concrete space, light glaring off its shiny industrial gray floor. The walls and ceiling were stark white. A row of skylight windows across the top of the back wall offered sunlight.

He daydreamed of dividing the space with a wall. The front would be the sales floor. The back would be his workshop. He'd leave the wall open a few feet across the top so that the light from the windows could still fill the entire space. He'd leave the floor the way it was but would paint each wall a different color to give each side some character, maybe put up some dividers to create small rooms.

He realized he'd need assistance to get all of this done in time. Some of his friends from the bar were good with construction and painting. If he offered to supply them with beer, they'd sign up. But he'd need assistance when Crosstown opened too. Maybe a part time employee to run the sales floor. Otherwise, when would he get any work done?

He'd never kept official store hours at his warehouse downtown. He came and went as he pleased and sold mostly to private clients. Moving to Crosstown would change all that. He'd always been his own boss and he liked that freedom, but now hiring someone seemed daunting. Did he use a staffing service or put an ad in a paper or something? How would he find someone he could trust?

Matthew needed help.

Chapter 31

Seraphina was free and decided to cash in an hour with Jaquan at Urban Oasis. She definitely wanted the massage, but she was also hoping to dish on Kyson.

"Girl, you crazy!" Jaquan said when she asked him.

"What?"

"Kyson is metrosexual maybe. He definitely ain't gay."

"But…the two of you were at Zoë's open house and went to Pipeline together afterwards."

"We are just friends! Please! He's new in town and I've just been showing him around. He is not my type. As for going to the gay bars, he likes the attention but at the end of the day he likes the ladies."

Seraphina fell quiet for a moment while Jaquan did some deep tissue work on her shoulders. When he was done, she spoke up again.

"Are you sure?"

"Positive."

"How do you know?"

"Um, I made him go to Pipeline, but in exchange he made me go to Platinum Plus!"

Platinum Plus was a local strip club in a purple-painted building.

"The Purple Church?"

"Is there any other one?"

Quiet again. Jaquan was working on her calves. Before he switched legs, she interrupted him.

"I can't wait to tell Zoë she was wrong."

"Zoë thought he was gay?"

"Zoë thinks everyone is gay," Seraphina said.

"Why did she think that?"

"Well…I…uh…I had a one night stand with him."

"And that makes him gay? What? You turning guys gay now?"

"No, silly!"

"Then what? I mean…he has a nice body and all, but lots of straight guys do."

"Don't tell him I told you this, but he was wearing a cheetah-print bikini thong," she whispered.

"A what?" Jaquan yelled.

"A bikini thong," she repeated a little louder.

"Oh my God! And that makes him gay?" Jaquan squealed.

"Shhh, not so loud. I don't want him to hear."

"Girl, he ain't here. He's gone to lunch."

"It was cheetah print."

"Was it sexy?" Jaquan asked with curiosity.

"Kinda. Don't tell Zoë I said that. Don't tell anyone I said that."

"Girl, you crazy! So you want to go out with him again?"

"We didn't go out."

"So you want to take him back to your place again?"

"How did you know we went to my place?" Seraphina asked.

"Umm…did I say that? I don't know. Now shh, let me finish your massage."

"But—."

He pushed her head back down into the head rest.

"Shh now! Massage!"

Chapter 32

Zoë immediately noticed Braden, or Brad as he reminded her, was not wearing a wedding ring. There was not even a tan line indicating he might have taken it off since he works with mulch and soil all day.

The Green Room was a quaint store front that served the public as a florist and garden shop. The store opened up into a large beautiful greenhouse that customers could walk through. Behind the shop were six other large greenhouses that were closed to the public and filled with plants and flowers grown and sold strictly to wholesalers.

Braden was much better looking than Brad Pitt in Zoë's

opinion. He had the quirky sex appeal of Billy Bob Thornton. His deep vibrato was reminiscent of Sam Elliot. He was at least a foot and a half taller than her, and very lean. She loved tall, skinny men for some reason, especially sexy ones.

His hair was short and silvery gray, as was his heavy five o'clock shadow. He had deep green eyes and a tiny sliver of a silver hoop earring that occasionally twinkled when the sun hit it just right. She wanted to nibble on his ear.

His hands looked surprisingly clean and there were no scars. She noticed slight calluses on the inside of his palms, a sign of hard work, but he wasn't the sweaty and dirty gardener one might have expected running this business. His clothes were clean and ironed; he wore a black apron over them. He smelled like sandalwood.

The more she walked around with him, the more he was becoming her new crush.

"So you want to learn about flowers?" he asked.

"Yes."

It wasn't an interview, but she couldn't think of anything else to say.

"What's your favorite flower?"

"Uhh…zinnias?"

"No it's not."

"No?"

"I bet you like dahlias. Or irises in the spring time."

"Sunflowers are nice," Zoë said, quickly going over all the flowers she could think of in her head.

She'd never heard of a dahlia. Roses seemed too predictable, though she did think they were pretty. Daisies were cute, but she couldn't remember if she'd ever smelled a daisy. Violets? Tulips? She couldn't think of anything else.

"Sunflowers *are* nice. What do you think of lilies?"

"What kind?" Zoë asked with a smile.

"Good question! Orientals?"

"Umm…do those include Stargazers?"

"Yes!"

"I like those. They smell nice."

"Yes, they do."

"What's your favorite?" Zoë asked.

"Probably depends on the time of year. You like calendulas?" he said.

"My face cream has calendula oil in it. Same thing?"

"Yep."

"I don't think I've ever seen one."

"Heard of marigolds?"

"Yes, my mother plants those."

"Same thing."

"Huh, I learned something today."

"So you mom is a gardener?" Brad asked.

"Yes. Vegetables, flowers, she grows a little of

everything."

"She the reason you are here today?"

"No, actually. I run a business in midtown that's in trouble, so I'm trying to learn something new. Reinvent myself. I was thinking of going into the flower business."

"What kind of business do you run now?"

"It's called Hands Across The Board. I sell local art."

"That place by The Blue Note in Overton Square?"

"Yeah, that's it."

"I've never been in there, but I've heard about the possibility of them tearing those buildings down. Is that why you are in trouble?"

"That's definitely the catalyst. Selling art has gotten tough over the years. People are more frugal with their money these days. I sell on commission too, so I want to start making more money for myself."

Brad listened intently, letting her speak.

"It's funny that you said people are getting frugal. That's true, but they'll still spend money on flowers. Makes them happy. It's traditional. They're pretty. They smell nice. It gets them outside and gives them something to tend to. They can watch them grow. They are signs of the seasons changing, of the weather getting warmer. And when they die, we don't mourn them. Yet, there's flowers at every funeral. Flowers mourn for us instead. Isn't that interesting?"

"I guess I never looked at them that way," Zoë said.

"Am I boring you?"

"What? No! Not at all! Honestly, and I don't mean to sound too bold or presumptuous, but I could listen to you talk all day and night."

"Oh yeah? I like bold."

"You do?"

"I don't mind presumptiveness either."

"You don't?"

"That's why you should have dinner with me some time."

"I should. I mean…I should?"

"You should."

Chapter 33

"Girl! Kyson ain't gay!" Seraphina sang to Zoë on the phone.

"What? How do you know?"

"Jaquan told me."

"But they were together at my open house."

"Just as friends."

"But Matthew knew him from the bar."

"Jaquan made him go there to hang out. He made Jaquan go to the titty bar with him."

"The titty bar? Maybe he's bi?"

"I don't think so. Jaquan said he definitely likes the ladies."

"Well, you know Jaquan better than I do. Guess he has no reason to lie or cover up for Kyson."

"You gonna hit on him now next time you get a massage?" Seraphina asked.

"Nope. I've got a date with someone else."

"Someone else? Who??" Seraphina screeched.

"Brad."

"From The Green Room?"

"That's the one."

"Is he as hot as he sounds on the phone?"

"Hotter!"

"You go, girl! When?"

"We haven't made plans just yet, but he asked me to dinner."

"Let me know when and I'll help you get ready."

"So, are *you* gonna hit on Kyson now?" Zoë asked.

"Honey, you know it! I already texted him!"

Chapter 34

After signing the paperwork and getting the keys, Matthew walked over to Pipeline. Brian was there. Marc wasn't. Matthew wasn't sure if he should mention his last meeting with Marc to Brian. Since Marc was drunk, he probably wouldn't even remember it, but it was hard for Matthew to forget.

"Hey, man," Brian said.

"Hey, Brian."

"What's up?"

"I just signed the lease on the new place at Crosstown."

"Congratulations! Want me to come by and christen it for

you?" Brian asked, winking at Matthew.

"Maybe."

"Maybe? What's wrong?"

"Can I ask you something?"

Matthew decided he'd just let it out.

"Sure," Brian said.

"Why did you and Marc break up?"

"What? Where's this coming from?"

"The night of the cruise, he was here."

"Did he piss you off?"

"A little."

"Was he drunk?"

"Yeah."

"He turns into a bitter queen when he's had too much to drink."

"Is that why you broke up?"

"Let's just say when you live with him he can be a queen even when he's sober."

"I see. Yeah, I don't think I want to hang out with him anymore though. Sorry."

"Really? Chances are he won't remember what he said."

"I'll remember."

"I get it. It's cool. We're still good, right?"

"Yeah, we're good. Wanna see my new shop?" Matthew asked with a grin.

They walked over to Crosstown. Brian was excited to see the inside of the old building.

"This place is amazing!"

"Isn't it?"

Since the place didn't have any furniture or walls yet, and there were too many construction workers passing by the outside, Matthew's new shop wasn't an ideal place to fool around.

They took the elevator up to look around at some of the upper levels. They found a dark stairwell leading up to the roof. It was the perfect place to make out. Pitch black.

With his jeans around his ankles, Matthew leaned back. He thought he was pressing against the wall but it was the door to the roof. It pushed open. He fell back and found himself lying on the roof of the warehouse, looking up at the Memphis sky.

"Are you okay?" Brian said, looking up at Matthew.

Matthew pushed Brian's head back down, smiling and not saying a word.

Chapter 35

"You thought I was gay?" Kyson asked Seraphina.

They'd been texting and decided to meet and grab a coffee at Starbucks.

"Sorry."

"Why didn't you just ask?"

"You were naked and in my bed."

"And that made you think I was gay?"

"It wasn't that."

"What was it then?"

Seraphina didn't want to say.

"You were with Jaquan at Zoë's shop."

"Just friends and we work together. He told you that."

"Matthew told us he knew you from Pipeline."

"Jaquan wanted me to go there. I made him go with me to the—."

Seraphina gave him a look.

"Sorry," he said. "Tell me why you thought I was gay."

"Okay. Okay. Don't hate me but it was the…cheetah print thong," she whispered the last three words.

"The what?"

"The cheetah print thong," she said a little louder.

"Huh?"

"The cheetah print thong!" she yelled.

A barista dropped a coffee cup and it smashed on the floor. The place fell quiet. Seraphina blushed.

Kyson started laughing.

"What?" Seraphina whispered.

Everyone in the café started talking again.

"Before I moved here, I was a stripper. Not a porn star. Just a stripper at clubs and private parties."

Seraphina gave him another look.

"Don't judge. It's good money. I never slept with the customers, if that's what you are thinking. Honest. But I was dating this girl and she got jealous and threw out all my things. So when I moved here, I didn't have much. That includes underwear. The thong was one of my stripper costumes."

"Seriously?"

"I told you I'm being honest. I can't believe you thought I was gay because of that! Ladies loved that thong."

"Oh, honey, no they didn't. If you stripped in a gay club here with that thong on, men would be all up on you."

"If it wasn't for Jaquan giving me a job, I'd probably be doing that. Gay men do tip better."

They went back to her place. He closed the door and she was on him as soon as he turned around. He slid his shirt off while kissing her. She unbuttoned his jeans.

"What are you wearing today?" she asked.

"No thong, that's for sure."

"Mmm, commando?" she asked, sliding them down.

"Sorry. I still haven't gone shopping."

"It's okay. Less things to take off. Saves time."

"What are you wearing under that dress?" Kyson asked, as he kissed her neck.

"Find out," she said, leading him to the bedroom.

Chapter 36

"No one else signed up for your class?" Zoë asked Brad.

After their meeting, she'd agreed to take his flower arranging class. He'd also agreed to teach her about selling flowers as part of her business.

"I do three classes a week. I reserved this one just for you," Brad said with a smile.

"You shouldn't have done that."

"Okay, I lied. I'm still teaching the other three classes. I created an extra class just for you."

"You just wanted to be alone with me," Zoë said.

"Does that make you mad?"

"No. I'm flattered. And overjoyed."

"You wanted to be alone with me too?"

"Yes, but arranging flowers is not what I had in mind."

"We could skip this part," Brad said, raising his eyebrows.

He was surprised she already knew how to properly cut stems and trim the leaves. She admitted she'd learned from her Mom and from her friend, Matthew.

"They taught you well."

"I did what she showed me, but a part of me believed she didn't know what she was doing either. She likes to pretend she knows."

"Don't ever underestimate your Mom."

"Are you kidding me? She definitely knows more than she says, thinks more than she speaks, and notices more than she fesses up to."

"I think I read that on a tee shirt once."

"She probably created it, licensed it, and sold it."

"And put it on a tee shirt! Are you like your mom?" Brad asked.

"In some ways, I suppose."

"Tell me how."

"She's a strong woman. Resilient."

"Is she as nice as you?"

"Are you kidding? She's mean as a bed of snakes."

"I find that hard to believe."

"I am kidding. She's my mom. She can be catty at times.

She's not afraid to put you in your place. But at the end of the day, she'll help. She'll feed you. She'd give you a place to stay if you needed it. Just take your shoes off before you walk through her clean house or you'll piss her off."

"I like her already," Brad said, laughing.

"She grew the flowers I sold at my open house, and she's paid the rent more than once when things were tight."

Brad stood beside Zoë as they each arranged a vase of flowers while they chatted. He talked her through it. He told her it was like painting a picture. There were no mistakes that couldn't be fixed. You could experiment with colors, sizes, and shapes.

"So tell me about you? Are you from here?" Zoë asked.

"Born and raised."

"Memphian through and through, huh?"

"Yep."

"What got you into flowers?"

"This was my mom and dad's business. Like your mom, they were tough. They worked hard. They liked helping others. My dad was the gardener. My mom arranged flowers and ran the store. Back then, it was just the store. Funeral homes and weddings were their main source of income. And Valentine's Day."

"Now I know why you have an entire greenhouse of just roses."

"Yeah, Valentine's Day is still a big day around here. But there's a lot of competition now. When I took over, I expanded the business to landscaping and other income to keep it going. More people in the city plant flowerbeds now or like to plant a small garden."

"It makes them happy. I never expected to sell all of my mom's flowers at the open house."

"And your arrangement there would make someone very happy."

"You think so?"

"I know so. And it would make me very happy if we had dinner tonight. You available?"

"I am."

"Pick you up at 6?"

"That would make me happy."

Chapter 37

He took her to a nice restaurant in Germantown which was east of Midtown and where all the nouveau riche lived. Zoë didn't spend much time in that area. Getting too close to the edge of Midtown made her nervous.

He'd worn a tie but she could tell it made him uncomfortable. She reached over at dinner and took it off for him. He thanked her and complimented her on how stunning she looked.

"Now what can I take off of you?" he said, teasing.

"You might get us kicked out."

"Somehow I don't think that would be a bad thing."

"You come here often?" she asked.

"Not really. You?"

"Never," she said with a laugh to let him know it was okay.

"Guess I should have just taken us to Huey's?"

Huey's was a popular burger joint in Midtown.

"That would have been okay with me."

"C'mon, let's get out of here."

"I hope you weren't trying to impress me."

"Nah, someone at work suggested it. I shouldn't have listened."

"That's okay."

"Tell me something I could learn from your mom?"

"How to gamble. She's really good at it."

"Really?"

"Yep. What about your mom? What could I learn?"

"How to arrange flowers, and I'm already passing that along to you. It's the best gift she ever gave me and I'm happy to share it."

"I like that."

He walked her to her door, having already let her know he wasn't going to come inside if that was alright.

"No need to rush things," he'd said. "I'm not going anywhere if you aren't."

She appreciated that and took his hand in hers as they walked up to her porch.

"Can I kiss you?"

"You don't even have to ask."

"Well, the only reason I did is because I'm much taller than you and I didn't want to end up kissing the top of your head."

"I'll meet you halfway."

And she did.

Brad had soft lips. Not too wet. Not too dry. She let him take control. She loved the feel of his arms around her waist. She wanted him to come inside and stay the night, but she too wanted to take time to enjoy this.

He left and Zoë went inside to call Matthew. She thought she might catch him before he went out for the night.

"I thought you had a date."

"I did. It's over."

"Didn't go so well?"

"No, it was amazing! He's such a gentleman."

"Are you falling in love?"

"Nah, I'm already there. It just feels right."

"I'm happy for you."

"Can I come over and we can work on some pottery again?"

"Of course. Your first piece is dry and ready to paint."

When she got to Matthew's place, he had already poured a glass of red wine for her. He laid out the paint and some brushes for them. She'd changed into a tee and jeans, but he gave her an apron to put on just in case she got sloppy with the paint.

"I want to ask you something," she said.

"Sure, ask away. Wait! Is this about Brad? Because you know I give horrible advice when it comes to relationships and dating and love. I'll just tell you what I know you want to hear."

"No, it's about Hands Across The Board," Zoë said.

"Oh, okay. What's up?"

"I've decided to close the shop. The future of Overton Square is bleak, which is the push I needed I suppose. But I wanted to ask what you think about—."

Matthew cut her off.

—about you being my business partner at Crosstown?" he said.

"Yes! How did you know?" Zoë asked, surprised.

"I guess we read each other's minds in a way. I had already planned on asking you. My shop downtown was never really an official retail space. I worked when I wanted to. I didn't see much traffic off the streets. But Crosstown will be much different. I need a shop manager, someone to run it on a daily basis."

"I can do that!"

"I know you can. So be my partner?" Matthew asked, sticking out his hand for her to shake.

"Okay!" Zoë said, taking his hand in hers.

"So how do we do this? What do you want to do? You wanna keep selling art on commission?"

"Not really. I want to sell my own art and yours too, of course. Maybe bring in a few of the higher end artists from my shop eventually, but not everyone and not right away either. We'll sell your furniture and do flowers too."

"So my furniture and art, with your art and flowers? I like it. We need a new name. What should we call the place?"

"How about…Encore?" Zoë said.

"Encore? I liked that!"

Encore. It was meant to be.

Chapter 38

Eviction notices in Overton Square were passed out a few weeks later notifying the businesses of what was to come. Zoë was gone before then, and so was Hands Across The Board.

She'd emailed all of the artists to let them know of her decision to close the shop and asked them to come by and pick up their art that was still there.

"Are you moving to Crosstown or somewhere else?" several asked.

"Are you going to open a new store?"

"Where will we sell our art?"

Everyone was full of questions again.

"I'll send an email and let everyone know if I have any opportunities for them," she said.

She didn't want to feel like she was pushing them out. She just wasn't sharing information yet. She didn't want anyone badgering her to sell their art at the new space. It would be a joint decision that she and Matthew would make together what commissioned art they sold, if any.

Hands had always been the artists' store. It had always been a place for them, a community. She was glad she could nurture that for as long as she did. Even though business had been slow the last few years, she was still proud of the place she'd provided for thriving local artists.

But now, she needed to do something for herself. She wanted to make this new space hers, and Matthew's. She wanted to sell her own art. She wanted to help Matthew be successful, and have him do the same for her.

She wasn't done.

An encore was needed. Encore felt right.

Chapter 39

Seraphina brought lunch for Zoë and Matthew as they put the finishing touches on Encore the day before the Crosstown Concourse's grand opening. They'd built some half walls on each side of the sales floor to create small rooms which were decorated to give customers ideas for their own homes. The floor was packed with pieces of Matthew's refurbished furniture. There were desks, chairs, storage cabinets, lamps, tables, plantstands, and more. Pieces of both of their pottery sat all around the store and were accented with flowers from Zandy's garden. There were also some house plants from The Green Room. Zoë had gotten quite good at using the potter's wheel and was proud of the pieces she had displayed now for sale.

There was a giant workstation in the middle of the store where Zoë could paint her pottery or work on a flower arrangement when she wasn't assisting customers. Just as Matthew had envisioned, a large wall divided the space to create a workshop for them in the back. It had been left open at the top to allow the sunlight from the back windows to filter over the sales floor.

The wall behind the workstation was covered with giant paintings of the city, pieces that they'd purchased up front from a few artists Zoë had worked with before. Zoë had found another artist who made blankets and rugs which were displayed throughout the store.

"This looks amazing," Seraphina said.

"Thanks," Matthew and Zoë both said.

"Congratulations, you two. I'm so excited. I've got a ton of clients that will be stopping by tomorrow."

"I'd like to speak to the manager," a voice said behind them.

It was Brad. He'd stopped by to see the store and say hello. He'd brought Zoë a gift.

"What's this?" she asked as she tore the paper off.

"You'll see," Brad said.

"Oh wow! How did you get this?"

It was a long, rustic wooden frame. Inside was a piece of fabric that said "Hands Across The Board." Zoë recognized it immediately. It was the fabric from the awning above the entrance to her old store.

"They're starting demolition on the Overton Square buildings. I figured the awnings would probably get trashed so I saved it and had this framed for you," Brad said.

"I love it!" Zoë said embracing him and giving him a long, passionate kiss.

"Alright, you two. Take it up to the roof," Matthew said.

"I thought that was your spot," Zoë teased.

Matthew blushed.

"The shop looks great," Brad said.

Zoë took him by the hand to show him around.

"She's so happy," Seraphina said to Matthew.

"Yeah, it's good to see this side of her for a change. It's been a while."

"What about you?" Seraphina asked.

"I'm happy too. How's things with Kyson?"

"Let's just say I'm definitely happy."

They both laughed.

"Are you two laughing at us?" Zoë said from across the store.

This made them laugh even more.

Chapter 40

The grand opening of Crosstown Concourse was spectacular. A crowd gathered for live music and several speakers, mostly city officials. When the ribbon was cut and people were allowed to go inside, Zoë and Matthew unlocked the doors to Encore and propped them open to welcome customers.

"I like the name," Zandy told Zoë.

"Thanks, Ma."

"It's easier to remember. One word. I could never remember the name of your other place. Do you know they tore it down?"

"I know. It's sad."

"But I love this new place. You've done well, Baby Girl."

"Thanks, Ma. And thanks for the flowers."

"Where's Matthew? I want to congratulate him."

"He's over there."

Zandy wandered off. Matthew gave her a hug and offered a glass of champagne.

"Wow! Look at all these people! Was that your Mom?" Brad asked, coming into the shop and greeting Zoë.

"That's Alexandra herself. She likes to be called Zandy."

"Want me to leave?"

"No, I'll introduce you."

Zoë was beaming with too much pride to worry about what her Mom might think of the man she was dating. Brad was a gentleman, and Zandy was polite but Zoë knew on the inside, she was judging him up and down.

"At least yours don't look like penises," Zandy said to Zoë when she showed her the pots she'd been making. "I love them. I'll take two."

"What are you going to do with them?" Zoë asked.

"My child made them so I'm going to pin them on the refrigerator. Maybe hang them on my Christmas tree. What do you mean? I'm going to put flowers in them, silly girl."

"So what do you think of Brad?" Zoë whispered.

"Brad's cute."

Zoë knew she approved. Zandy had always been a woman

of few compliments.

"Thanks again for coming to the grand opening, Ma. I love you."

"I love you too, dear. So is this the new you?"

"What do you mean?"

"You're glowing. You seem happy. Is Brad good to you?"

"I am happy, Ma. And yes, he's good to me."

"Bring him with us to the casino next time."

"Okay, we'll do that."

Seraphina stopped by with Kyson. She delivered some business cards that she'd had made for Zoë and Matthew. Jaquan was there too and bought a side table.

"No jokes about this being my new side piece," he said to Matthew.

"Speaking of side pieces," Zoë said, noticing Brian and Marc walking in together.

"Do I need to get the hose?" Jaquan said.

"I'm fine," Matthew said.

Brian and Marc were apparently back together. This let Matthew know that everything Brian had told him was just so he could mess around with him again. Matthew didn't have much to say to either of them, but they did buy an eight hundred dollar dining table and six chairs that Zoë sold them.

"Nicely done," Matthew whispered to Zoë.

"You know you're still going to sleep with them," she said,

with her hand on her hip.

"Eh, probably. Doesn't mean I can't be a bitch to them for a while."

"You learned from the best, Baby," Zoë said.

"Who? Seraphina?"

"Ah! You are a bitch!" Zoë said, pinching his arm.

They mingled with their customers and friends, showing them the new shop. Several of Zoë's artist friends stopped in to say hello and congratulate her. No one mentioned Hands Across The Board to her, which was now a cleared space of land awaiting its uncertain future. It didn't matter. Today was a new day for Zoë.

"These flowers came from my very own garden. Yes, homegrown right here in Memphis," Zandy was telling one of the customers.

"Ma, what are you doing?"

"Selling stuff. Tell Matthew to put me on your payroll."

"We will if you buy breakfast for us next time we go to Tunica," Zoë joked.

"Can we take Frampton's car?" Matthew asked.

"Is there any other way to go?"

At the end of the night, they celebrated their successes with a drink at Pipeline. Crosstown was finally open. Encore was up and running. It was a new page, a new chapter, for both Matthew and Zoë.

As Zoë recalled the evening and all of the people she'd spoken to, she remembered a question someone had asked. She couldn't remember who had said it to her or when. Maybe it was Seraphina. Maybe it was her mother or Brad. Or maybe it was an old customer of hers or one of the artists she'd done business with before.

"Are you going to enjoy being on this new side of things?" they'd asked.

What did they mean by this side of things? Maybe they meant this side of town. Crosstown was still in Midtown but a mile or so from Overton Square where her old shop had been. Or maybe they meant being the artist herself and selling her own stuff instead of everyone else's.

She was probably overthinking it. She did not even remember how she had responded to them. It didn't matter. She was going to be okay. She liked this new side of things, being in this new place, and dating someone new too.

She liked this new side of herself just fine.

A note from the author:

I've always been intrigued by the long list of names an author includes in their thank you note at the end of a book, pages of names I usually just scheme over. What did all those people do?

Writing, for me, has always been a very personal and lonely process, but I like it that way. It's the solitary time I get to spend with my story and my characters as I create it, before I'm done with them and release them into the world to meet other people and to be judged by my literary merit.

As I've often said and written, writing is a lot like having an affair with a secret lover. You want them all to yourself. You don't want anyone to know about them, at least not for a while.

Even now as I write this closing note, I can count on one hand the number of people who even know about this book and I'd have fingers left over. And no one has even read a word of it yet. But that will change between now and when the book is actually published so I suppose I do at least have some people to thank.

Zoë would not exist if it weren't for the woman she is based upon, Lois, who was my dear coworker and friend during my days living in Memphis. We met in 1997 and though it seems like we knew each other much longer, I left Memphis in late 2001 and we fell out of touch. I miss her dearly, but have managed to still be a part of her life, and she has been a part of mine, thanks to the wonders of social media.

Back then, I always knew I was going to write a book. She told me to put her in the book and call her Zoë, so that's just what I did in 2003 when I wrote *The Other Side of What*.

Lois taught me how to have fun. She taught me how to have compassion. She also gave good advice, though I was reckless when it came to listening to it. I tried very hard to pay her back my representing her character, honesty, and passion through Zoë. I often wonder if I taught her anything all those years ago.

Once I write a book, a few years pass before I write anything else. I never thought of writing a sequel until someone once asked me about a character in my second book, *Stealing Wishes*, published in 2008. That inquiry led to a sequel, *Feeling Himself Forgotten*, published in 2016. And now, I find myself in the exact same situation again.

On June 25th, 2019 Lois's real-life daughter messaged me through social media inquiring about which of my books her mother appeared in. I was happy to answer her questions, but this got me to thinking about where Zoë might be now. I sat down the next day at my computer to find out and now here we are. Thanks Jessica!

I also owe a big thanks to Niambi, Louis's best friend. I asked her who she would be if she was a character in a book, and Seraphina was the answer.

Through the process of writing this book, I discovered that I like writing novellas, and I thoroughly enjoyed catching up with Matthew and Zoë now sixteen years later. So, there might be "other sides" of more characters to come.

I told you I'd have fingers left over, so thank you for reading.

Shannon Yarbrough

July 26, 2019

Other Books by Shannon Yarbrough:

The Other Side of What

Stealing Wishes

Are You Sitting Down?

Dickinstein

Feeling Himself Forgotten